"I love you, Allen," she admitted and took his face in her hands. He kissed her, slightly at first, his lips lingering upon hers. Then with more urgency, he pressed past her lips to find her tongue. She moaned loudly. A sensation inside of her awakened — one she had never felt before — and she wrapped her arms about his neck, pulling him closer to her. She could feel the hardened length of him strain against the cloth that separated them, that kept them from being one.

Indigo Sensuous Love Stories

Genesis Press, Inc.
315 Third Avenue North
Columbus, MS 39701

Unfinished Love Affair

ISBN: 1-58571-074-1
Manufactured in the United States of America

First Edition

Acknowledgments

I have to give thanks to my God, Almighty, and his Son, Jesus Christ, from whom all my blessings flow. To my mom, my brother and his family for their unending love and support; my cronies, who continuously root me on - I'm going to start calling yall the AMEN corner! To my fellow-sister-girls: Rochelle Alers, Natalie Dunbar, Gwen Forster, Donna Hill, BJ Woodbury-what would a sister like me do without love and support from sisters like yall?! To all the book store managers, especially Bridget at Waldenbooks in Ford City Mall; all the book clubs and those who bought my first book and this one. Without your support all of this is for naught! And lastly, to Wynelle Claudette Bush Wilson-your love, your ideas, your support, your true sister-friendship, as well as your taking the time to read my work and offer real, insightful criticism is a true blessing! Thank you!

This book is dedicated to the late
Sherrie Barnett Brock Parker.
May your spirit soar and live on forever. Amen.

Prologue

"How can you say that to me, Allen?!" Kayla cried, her face red as a blistering inferno. She crossed her arms about her, in a hug of shock and denial, then sank on the couch. "When did all of this happen?" She asked, gasping for air, her head spinning, not giving him a chance to answer. "So, I guess what you've been telling me, how much you love me, is one big lie?!"

Allen grimaced and attempted to stare past the pain in her eyes. In the nearly three years that they had dated, he had never seen Kayla this angry. When they had met that summer, which seemed to Allen like a lifetime ago, it was her cool demeanor and an unspoken passion for life which shone through her eyes that initially attracted him to her. And what's more, it didn't hurt that he found her one of the most beautiful women he'd ever seen. From her shoulder length sun-streaked brown hair, to her round clear cocoa-colored eyes complemented by her mocha-smooth skin, he was taken. Yet, he couldn't shake the unmistakable fear that gripped him with each passing day. At twenty-seven, Allen didn't feel as if he were ready for the type of commitment he knew Kayla sought. Marriage just wasn't in his plans.

"Kayla, I'm just not ready for marriage," he sighed. "I'm not the man for you." He bowed his head to shield his eyes. "I . . . I don't love you." There! He'd said it, but he also knew he was lying. He felt he had to, for in his mind the type of love Kayla had given him, the warmth and rightness of their relationship just didn't exist. He didn't want to believe it existed. And he was determined not to let the voice in his heart tell him otherwise. He straightened. "We can't be together anymore, Kayla."

She turned. Then refocusing her eyes, she saw Allen's version of the truth spread across his handsome face. Slowly, with the backs of her hands, she wiped at the tears that had begun to flow freely. In her short twenty-two years, she had never cried in front of anyone outside of her father and sister — and it had been some time since she'd done that. As she thought about it, how she must look, she became angry. Angry at the pride she had lost for the sake of the love of some man. Never again.

She rose and headed to the door. Pausing there, she turned to look at Allen, resolve and uncertainty wrestling in his warm brown eyes, then across his face. She looked away, opened the door and walked out.

Allen watched her go. He wanted to call her back, wanted to see her eyes minus the pain he had witnessed moments earlier. Too late. Something inside of him said it would be a long time before he saw her beautiful face again. He shrugged his shoulders. What was done, was done and he knew it.

Kayla's mind replayed him standing there, his hands shoved into the front pockets of his jeans, as he told her they were finished, that he didn't love her any longer. At first, she didn't want to believe what she was hearing, for just two days ago, they were laughing and loving, wrapped up in each other's arms. There had been no clue — no clue as to the words he would speak to her, the actions he would take to erase her from his life. In her mind, their relationship was secure and she was looking forward to a proposal of marriage. Sure she had been the one to broach the subject — Allen had been her first, and she couldn't see loving or making love to another man. She had given him her gift — a gift she wanted to save for the man she married, the man whom she would bear children for, share all her dreams with. That man, so she thought, was Allen. Now, with startling insight, she realized she had been the only one who broached the subject of marriage. Allen had always nodded his head and looked away.

"This is a really sick joke," Kayla said to herself as she hurried down the street, her thoughts tumbling over the last hour's events. Then the tears she had shed came back with a vengeance. Her shoulders convulsed with each tear drop, and she cried openly. She had never experienced pain like this. Even when the realization that her mother wouldn't be returning had hit her so many years before, she hadn't felt like dying — hadn't felt as if the world could just swallow her up whole and she wouldn't care.

This wasn't real, she tried to tell herself, it can't be real.

The earlier mist, which had floated gently from the clouds, had turned to torrents of heavy rain, leaving her jeans and shirt soaking wet and sticking cruelly to her skin.

Kayla stopped at a corner and looked up at the street sign. She had walked for nearly fifteen blocks before she realized where she was. She knew a bus stop wasn't far and headed in that direction.

As she waited for the bus, she wiped the tears that had mixed with the warm rain drops from her face and vowed never again to set eyes on Allen Dawson.

For weeks thereafter, Kayla sequestered herself in her room. She cried continuously, her pillows streaked with the evidence of her pain. She had found it hard to eat, and sleep evaded her — and when sleep did come, it was always accompanied with various dreams of Allen. When she dared look in a mirror, she hated what she saw — a gaunt version of who she had been before and during Allen. He had become an integral part of her life, had been everything to her and the memory of their lovemaking caused her body to ache.

The images of the first time they made love slammed headfirst into her mind, creating a vortex she wasn't able to shake. But oh, it had been so sweet. The roof top of Allen's building. The warmth of that Indian summer night. The lights which shone in his eyes. The sweet sensation that enveloped her when he entered her. Her first orgasm. The soft, whispered words of love. The song "Sensuality," that played as they made love. It was all so very succulent. She knew she had found her soul mate.

"Are you sorry?" Allen had asked, his tone solicitous.

"No, Allen, I didn't think this would be so beautiful."

He sighed. "When you love someone, it is beautiful."

"Allen?"

"Yeah, baby girl."

"I will love you forever."

What had gone wrong, she wondered for what seemed like the millionth time since their breakup. What had happened to them?

The voice of her sister snapped her back into the present. "Kayla." She heard Laura call her name, her voice soft, but stern. "Kayla, baby, open the door."

Kayla forced the memory away, then pulled her body up heavily from her position on the bed. She had hidden from Laura and her father long enough. In fact, she had stewed in her own pity party long enough.

"Yeah," Kayla replied, her voice came out raspy and barely audible. "Come on in." She unlocked, then opened the door, wiping a single tear from her smooth cheek, plopping back on the bed.

"Hey, baby girl," Laura said, calling her by the name their father had given her. "You've been in here long enough." She sat on the edge near Kayla's head and began to lightly stroke her hair. She gently pulled Kayla's face upward to look into her eyes. "I know you're hurt, but it's time to get out and live again."

"Laura," Kayla began, a fresh flood of tears accompanying her words. "I loved him. I've never loved anyone like that before."

Laura took Kayla into her arms and rocked her. She wanted to kill Allen, wanted him to hurt as much as her baby sister was hurting. She vowed not to tell Kayla that Allen had been calling daily since their break up. He said that he was just checking on her. But she would kill him before she let him speak to her. No, Laura felt that the last thing Kayla needed was to speak to him again, to hear his voice. She had to get over him. What was done, was done, and it was time for her to move on.

Even though Laura knew her younger sister was no longer a child, she felt responsible for her; more so after their mother left them to chase some wild dream. "I know, Kayla. I know," she comforted, "but life has to go on. Sure, when you love someone and that someone doesn't return your love, it hurts. It hurts something fierce. But the fact that you loved Allen shows that you can love. And you can love again. You might not think so now, but give it time — you'll see."

Kayla shrugged as she rose from the bed, her hand firmly in Laura's. She loved her sister for caring so much. But in her heart there was no way she could ever forget. There was no way she would ever be the same. Ten years could pass, she told herself, and she would never love again.

Chapter 1

"Jonathan, what is it now?" Kayla breathed out heavily. Twice a week for the past six months Jonathan had made it his personal business to call her. Kayla saw right through him. She knew he was fishing to find out if there was anyone special in her life. And though there wasn't, she wasn't going to admit it to Jonathan, especially not him, her ex-husband.

"I just wanted to know how you're doing, Miss Martin?" He sighed. "Can't a brother check on the love of his life?"

"Not if you're trying to get me to go out with you, Jonathan."

Kayla pushed her hair behind her ears, her eyes mere slits under her long lashes as she gazed out of the living room window of her tenth floor loft overlooking Wabash Avenue. She wiggled her slender toes, the nails painted a bright fuschia, and stifled a sad laugh. She had long given up on her ex-husband. They had married nearly ten years ago and hadn't even made it to the five-year mark. The first year had been sweet. Jonathan showered her with his undivided attention. When year two slipped upon them, she began to notice the change, first in him, then in herself. At the three-year mark, she finally came to the hurtful realization that they had married each other on the rebound.

They had met following disastrous long-term relationships. Hers was with Allen and Jonathan's was with his high school sweetheart, Serena.

When Kayla divorced Jonathan, nearly seven years earlier, she knew she had married him more out of fear of not wanting to be alone and less for love. She even felt that maybe Jonathan shared her same feelings. They had come together at a time when each was feeling unloved and unwanted. The solace, no matter how short, served them both at a point in their lives when they needed it most. Kayla grimaced. That's what rebounding does. But now things were different, and Kayla felt she no longer needed, nor wanted the fleeting solace Jonathan once represented. Still, she felt guilty for not having been and still not being completely honest with him.

"So, sweetheart, you still passing out D's and F's?" Jonathan joked, changing the subject. Kayla was relieved. Even though she knew that it was past the time to come clean about her feelings for him, there was something that kept her from doing so.

"Jonathan, you know I don't give out those types of grades," Kayla laughed, stretching out on her deep plum colored chemise. She resolved to let Jonathan play out his feeble attempt to nose into her personal life. "Besides, a student would have to completely fail to show up and do absolutely nothing but stare at the walls to get those types of grades out of me."

Kayla thought of her seven-year tenure and her many students at East-West University. She liked teaching creative writing, enjoyed the opportunity to share her knowledge, as well as gain some herself — the simple sharing of consciousness, then turning it into something creative, was a part of her passion.

At thirty-two, she couldn't dream of a better job. She taught four classes a semester, counseled students, and conducted an after school workshop for high school students. And then there was the added asset of the summers off. She could do exactly what she wanted when she wanted. She smiled broadly at that thought, for it was last summer that her first book was published. It had been a lifelong dream to write and have published the story of the amazing black nuns, the Oblate Sisters of Providence, who had dedicated their lives to the teaching of black children. Kayla herself was a product of those great women's love and dedication in grammar school, and though she admitted that they were tough, she came to love and respect their dedication to excellence.

Yes, she mused to herself, life was going well. Now, if she could just get Jonathan to move on with his life, maybe all would be right.

"Well, that's good to hear," he replied. "So, are you breakin' hearts? You know you're a heart breaker."

"Oh, please, Jonathan," she huffed, then pictured him lounging on the black leather sofa in the den of the home they once shared, his long legs splayed out in front of him, the phone nestled in the crook of his neck. "Why don't you just spit it out? You want to know if I've found someone else."

They were both silent. Kayla thought of the last man she had dated. A good looking bronze-colored brother, with beautiful hazel eyes, Danny had turned into a real life nightmare. His insistence on knowing her exact whereabouts was disturbing. And when he had popped up, uninvited, lurking among the shadows near her loft, she knew she had to get rid of him — fast.

"Always, Jonathan. Always." Kayla joked. "Why do you want to know?"

"As I said, I'm just checking up on you, that's all."

"Well, how's Serena and Jovanna?" Kayla smiled at the question. She knew it was her ace in the hole that would move Jonathan out of his fantasy of their getting back together and back to the reality of his own current situation. She could picture his near midnight black eyes squinting at the inquiry.

"Jovanna is great. She'll be six this year."

"What about Serena?" Kayla asked snidely.

"We broke up," he said softly.

Kayla wasn't in the least bit sorry. She figured that's what Serena deserved for messing with a married man. When she had found out that Jonathan was not only having an affair with Serena, but had fathered her child, her decision to file for divorce was made easier. She didn't have to stand in front of the judge and admit that she married Jonathan out of fear and insecurity, that she really didn't love him. Unbeknownst to Jonathan, his infidelity provided her with the perfect excuse.

She laughed sadly at that last thought. It wasn't fair. She hadn't been fair. Following her break up with Allen, she was lost and hurt. In her mind, she just knew she and Allen would be together; she had planned on them living out their lives as one, making dreams come true. But as the old Jewish proverb goes, "Man plans and God laughs." And boy, did God laugh.

"Jonathan, I really must go. I'm having lunch with my dad and I don't want to be late."

"How is Joseph?"

Kayla sighed loudly. Jonathan was beginning to grate on her last nerve, and she reserved her last nerve for herself. "He's fine."

"And Laura?"

"Look Jonathan," Kayla barked. "They're both well. I've got to go now. Take care." And she hung up. Some days, she wondered why she accepted any of his phone calls. She berated herself for not having a nonpublished number. Then again, all she had to do was ask him to stop calling, but upon further thought, she wondered if her reluctance to do so stemmed from her own selfishness. Was she trying to prove to Jonathan that she was doing well, that she was making it in spite of the turmoil? But the turmoil wasn't his fault and it was at times like this that she had to question her own character. She hadn't loved him, still didn't. He had been a diversion, her escape from the realities of a love gone wrong. He deserved better — he deserved a woman who would love him, totally and without reserve, and she hadn't done that. She had just clung to him out of desperation. None of it was right, and she knew it. Even after ten years, the sudden break up with Allen still hurt, maybe not as bad as it had that first year, but the pain still simmered.

Kayla shrugged her shoulders, stretched, then stood. Her cat, General Patton, stretched with her. "Time to get dressed," she said absently to Patton as she reached to scratch behind its ears.

In the shower, Kayla thought of Allen. It had been a long time since she had seen him, ten years to be exact, and she often found herself wondering how he was doing, if he had met anyone special. Oh, she knew he wasn't married; his brother, Tim, had said so. Tim was her mechanic, his skills second to none, and she didn't understand, with all of his talent, why he hustled for a living — why he didn't take those skills and open up his own shop. She knew he could be rich ten times over by now.

She thought about the deal they had made. He was to repair her car, for which she payed him handsomely, as long as they didn't discuss Allen. Still, every once in a while, Tim would let slip the fact that Allen wasn't in a relationship. Other than those occasional slips, they both kept to their word. Yet, it was those very slips that stirred her memory of Allen's tender touch.

Kayla had walked around in a complete daze for months thereafter. But what disturbed her most were the dreams. She couldn't forget those dreams. Even after her heart began to heal, the explicit dreams of him holding her close, his hands splaying the length of her hair, haunted her.

Actually, when she truly thought about it, she couldn't seem to shake the feelings that there were words left unsaid — that there was some unfinished business between them.

She stepped out of the shower and headed to her bedroom.

"Some things are better left unsaid," Kayla spoke to her reflection in the mirror on her closet door.

She stood for a long moment, wrapped in a large lilac bath towel, and studied herself. Sure, there had been plenty of dates over the years, some she would just as soon forget, but none had ignited any passion, made her feel as special as Allen had. He had been so attentive, always picking up small gifts for her. Forget me nots, he had called them. And he seemed to know exactly what she liked. He knew she wasn't into showy pieces and grandiose items. She liked simple things.

Kayla looked over her shoulder at the crystal cat that sat on her night stand near a picture of herself and her family. It was the last gift Allen had given her.

"What went wrong?" she asked herself the same question she had so many times before. No matter how much she thought, analyzed the scene, she still came up with the same conclusion: Allen did not love her.

Kayla shook her head slightly, dismissing her thoughts, then began to dress. She pulled her hair back into a pony tail, deciding to forgo hot-curling it. She grabbed her fur trimmed black leather coat, then placed her black beret on her head, adjusting it to just the right angle. She stopped to check her appearance, nodded her approval and rushed out of the door.

Chapter 2

Kayla gunned the accelerator on her brassy red Toyota Solara, switched the gear to its top speed, and whipped around the slower moving cars on State Street. She glanced at the LED clock on the console. She had told her father, Joseph, that she would meet him at Red Fish Restaurant at one o'clock. It was now ten minutes to, and she was at least another fiteen minutes away.

She breezed through two caution lights. Then, caught at the third one, she watched absently as people rushed across the intersection of Randolph. A light snow had started to fall, and though it hadn't begun to accumulate, Kayla liked watching it fall. As a matter of fact, just before Jonathan's monthly intrusive phone call, she had been sitting in the large picture window of her loft watching dreamily as the light flakes drifted downward, many leaving wet droplets on the window. The month of March had swept in with a blizzard, and just like most of Chicago's weather, it was a month of unpredictable cold and snow.

"Sorry dad," Kayla apologized and kissed her father on the cheek. She sat down across from him and studied his warm features. At seventy, Joseph didn't look a day over forty. With the exception of the triangular patches of gray at

his temples, his head was full of jet black curls. She hadn't
inherited the curls, but instead she had gotten her mother's
thick long hair.

"That's okay, baby girl," he patted her hand. "I knew you
were on your way." Kayla smiled at the pet name her father
called her by. It was the one phrase that would sooth her, his
deep baritone voice resonating on each word.

The pair sat and chatted endlessly, their conversation
roaming across every subject, but when they came to
Jonathan, Kayla became silent.

"Is he still calling?"

"Yup," Kayla responded as the waiter set a large bowl of
Jambalaya in front of her. She bowed her head in prayer,
picked up the spoon, then dipped it in the dish, her eyes cast
downward. "He called me today."

"Umph. Do you ever hear from that Allen boy?"

Her head snapped upward. What would make him ask
about Allen, she thought. Her father hadn't brought up his
name in years. Why now, she wondered.

"No, daddy, I haven't heard from Allen in quite some
time. It's been at least ten years."

"Well, I heard from Jeanette the other day."

"Oh?" she began, trying to rid her voice of any emotion.
"What did she want?"

"She's coming to the states in May. Said she wants to
come home," he responded. Kayla looked into her father's
deep set, expressive brown eyes. Her mother had left them
twenty years ago with no explanation. Jeanette was just shy of

her eighteenth birthday when she married Joseph, and had been young and ill prepared for a family, but to Kayla this didn't offer any viable reason for running off to some foreign land with a man nearly fifteen years her junior. Her abandonment had caused Kayla to consider her dead.

"Well now, isn't that special?" Kayla replied snidely. She wasn't quite sure she wanted to see her mother. It had been five years since she last spoke with her, damn near twenty since she last laid eyes on her. Now here her father was telling her she was coming home. What home? She left them, so as far as Kayla was concerned, Jeanette had no home to come to. "Where is she planning on staying?"

Joseph sighed loudly. "At the house."

"You've got to be joking?" Her thick eyebrows rose.

"I wish I was, baby girl. She'll be here the second week of May."

"Have you told Laura?"

"No, not yet. I'm trying to find the right time to tell her."

Kayla nodded in agreement. Her sister was the feisty one in the family. Three years older, and the spitting image of Jeanette, Laura had taken on the complete responsibility of running the house and raising Kayla after her disappearance. It was her rule that no references to Jeanette were ever to be made.

"That may be wise. How do you feel about her returning?" Kayla looked at her father.

"I'm not sure. But I was surprised, to say the least."

They finished their meal in silence. When Joseph walked her to her car, he kissed her lightly on the cheek, then pulled her into a warm embrace. She smiled as she inhaled his cologne, Alfred Sung for Men, and rested her head on his chest. She liked the fragrance. It was the one pleasant memory of Allen that didn't unnerve her. It was his signature cologne, and outside of her father, no man had ever smelled better wearing it.

"Dad?" Kayla reluctantly pulled out of her father's secure embrace. "Wait until Laura's back from her vacation to tell her. Okay?"

"Okay," Joseph replied, then took his daughter by the hand and helped her into her car. He shut the door and poked his head in the window. "You be careful, and I'll talk to you tomorrow." He waved.

Kayla's head spun. There was just no way she could fathom Jeanette's return. After all this time, she wanted to come home, and act like they were all one big happy family. NOT! There would be no homecoming, no happily ever after. There would be no hugs and kisses, no words of love and forgiveness. No! Kayla had resolved that chapter in her life, just like she had those involving both Allen and Jonathan. Onward, not backward was her motto.

Following lunch and Joseph's unnerving news, Kayla wasn't in the mood to just go home and sit. Instead, she decided to park her car at the loft, retrieve the papers from the writing classes she taught, then take a cab to the University.

For three hours Kayla read paper after paper. Once she finished with those, she spent another hour and a half planning her syllabus for the Fall Semester. And though it was approximately five months away, drafts were due to the dean of the English Department no later than June first.

Satisfied, she rubbed her eyes, then stretched. She blinked at the darkened sky visible outside her office window and frowned. The earlier light snow had turned to heavy flakes, then icy cold sleet. As she stood to gather her belongings, her cell phone rang.

"Hello," she said into the receiver.

"Hey, girl! Where are you?" her best friend and OES sister, Amina, said excitedly. Kayla laughed at the singsong way she always greeted her.

"I'm just leaving the office. Why?"

"Meet me at Java Oasis."

"Sure, what time?"

"I'm heading there now. Come on." Amina disconnected, as always, without a goodbye.

Kayla put on her coat and beret, grabbed her leather satchel and rushed out the door.

Chapter 3

Kayla bristled as she pulled the collar of her jacket up around her neck. Oh yeah, Chicago's biting cold wind was in full effect. She smiled in spite of the blistering wind and sleet that whipped around her as she stepped out of the building and onto the side walk.

Bowing her head against it, she made her way over to the curb, bumping into several people, each like the other, all scurrying to get out from under Chicago's "hawk."

She raised her hand again, signaling a cab, then suddenly jumped backward as it slid to the curb causing a large puddle to wash over her entirely, leaving her drenched from head to toe in icy, muddy, grey water. Kayla squinched her eyes, inhaled deeply, then opened the passengers' door of the cab. She leaned her head into the vehicle and went into a verbal tirade, ending her assault with a few choice words of profanity before she kicked the cab door shut.

"Well, I guess he'll watch where he's going from now on," an amused voice said from behind her.

She put her hands on her hips and twirled around. "And you have an opportunity to stay ..." Her voice trailed off as she faced the voice. "Allen?!"

She was stunned. Here he stood, smiling at her, his boyishly handsome face etched in her memory.

"Yes, in the flesh." He smiled. "It's been a long time. How have you been?" He took Kayla's hand, pulled her into his large arms, then hugged her tightly.

It was still the same — inviting, suggestive and safe. And he was wearing Alfred Sung! Imagine that. The very scent that used to wreak havoc with her senses. But no more! She freed herself discreetly from his arms, and for an instant struggled with the temptation to grab him by his collar and slap him smartly across his face. Did he really think she had forgiven him? That all was well between them? She wondered. She may have gotten over him, but she sure as hell hadn't forgotten or forgiven.

Allen led her to the side of the building, his six-foot-one inch frame towered over her. "It's so good to see you Kayla. How have you been?"

She bit her bottom lip. Sure, ten years had come and gone — how did he think she was? Sitting at home, pining over him? Not! "Just fine, Allen. Working hard, but I'm fine."

"I'll say."

"What did you say?" Kayla shivered. She had hoped he would get the hint and let her move on — move out of his searing zone, one that caused an undeniable heat, and back to her own safe one. To Kayla, conversation of any kind with Allen was definitely not in her game plan today, or any other day for that matter. Still, she was incredulous. This had to be some sick dream. Allen?! Allen Dawson?!

The day was really full of surprises. First Jonathan's phone call, followed by the news of her mother's return to Chicago, now her bumping, literally, into Allen.

"You remember that old camp phrase, don't you? You say 'I'm fine,' and I say: 'I know you are.'"

She laughed in spite of herself. It was one of the many silly, yet endearing phrases he used when they were together. She had to admit that she liked them back then. Even now, it still sounded sweet coming from him.

"Still charming I see," she responded and began to walk away. She glanced at her watch. Kayla knew that if she hurried she would be able to at least make the second performance of a Jazz trio playing at the little coffee house she and Amina frequented most Saturday nights.

"Where are you on your way to?" Allen easily matched Kayla's gait.

"Well, I was on my way to meet my friend," she said, then looked down at the water dripping from her leather coat. "But now it looks like I'm going home to change."

He took her gently by the arm. "Come on, let me give you a ride."

Kayla freed herself. "That's not necessary, Allen. I can get a cab."

"No, Kayla," he demanded, then chuckled. "Besides, as you just witnessed, cabs are not the way to go this evening, and driving you home will give me a chance to play catch up."

She looked into his eyes. He had the warmest brown eyes she had ever seen, a rich chocolate which sparkled when he laughed. They were different though, oh the color was the same, but they seemed to hold a sadness — a longing of sorts. She dismissed the thought and contemplated the offer.

"Play catch up, huh?"

"Yes," he looked at her, the slight wrinkles in his forehead creating two single lines. "It's been a long time. Where are you living now? Same place?"

"No, I moved out years ago. I live on South Wabash."

"Great. My car is just around the corner here in the parking garage."

Kayla gave in. She was cold and wet, and a ride in a warm car was much more inviting than trying to hail a ride in a cab. The pair scurried around the corner and headed toward the parking garage. On the short walk, Kayla began to feel odd — the whole incident was something out of a made-for-tv drama.

A decade had flown by since she last saw him. Even in a city as big as Chicago you're bound to run into old flames now and then, but this hadn't happened to them. And that was just fine with her.

The parking attendant was waiting when they arrived.

"Thanks, Tommy," Allen said to him. "I'll see you next week."

"Got cha, chief. You have a good night," the attendant replied, handed Allen the keys then opened the passenger door.

Next week? She wondered. What was Allen doing downtown?

He glanced at her, saw the question in her eyes. Not yet. He hoped he'd get the opportunity to show her. "Wait a second." Allen stopped Kayla. "I've got a jacket in the back." Retrieving it, he held it toward her. "Here, put this on." Without protest from Kayla, he removed her wet leather coat, then slipped his coat about her shoulders, his eye catching a glimmer from the gold charm bracelet she wore around her slender wrist. "I was taking it to the cleaners."

She laughed as the charcoal-grey wool coat dwarfed her five-foot even frame. He smiled at the sound of her laughter. God, how he'd missed her.

Kayla whistled at the sleek black sedan as she settled into the warmth of its matching black leather seats. Allen shut her door, climbed into the driver's seat and put the car in gear.

"Wow," she began. "This is nice."

"You like?"

"Yeah. How long have you had it? It still smells like its new."

"I got it about six months ago. Actually, I got it for a steal. I bought it at one of those auctions. Imagine getting a Mercedes at an auction?" Allen laughed. "My brother, Tim. You remember him. Don't you?" He watched her reaction, saw none, then continued when she nodded her head. "The on again, off again mechanic? Well, he took me to one, checked out the car from bumper to bumper and here it is."

"May I ask how much you paid?"

"You can." He smiled broadly. "I paid nineteen for it."

"Nineteen?! That's a steal."

"Told you." Allen tapped his fingers on the steering wheel.

His wide, even smile was the same, she thought as she studied him like she was seeing him for the first time. It only made his good looks look even better. She noted that he seemed to have put on a little weight, which actually complemented his well-built frame, and wondered if his arms were still as muscular as they used to be, his chest broad and wide. Kayla admonished herself for allowing thoughts of a barely clad Allen to roam shamelessly through her mind.

As he talked, she looked him over — the same slightly full lips, a mustache trimmed to perfection, a pugged nose adding to his handsome features. The longer she watched him the warmer she became. Her body began to remind her that it had been a long time since she had felt the comfort of a man, the comfort of strong hands to caress her lovingly. She shook her head. Get a grip, she chided herself.

He interrupted her thoughts. "You better tell me now what your address is. You know me, I'll get to running my mouth and take you home with me."

Kayla ignored his last statement. "I live at 1710 South Wabash."

"You live in those fancy lofts?"

"Yeah, I've been there for about six years."

"They're really improving that area. Now, it's my turn. What did you pay for it?"

Kayla chuckled. "As you say 'I got it for a steal.' It was the model unit and they were having a hard time getting rid of it. It had two great views and one really bad one. The patio off the master bedroom looked right over into a junk yard."

"And let me guess, you didn't mind the junk yard?"

"Actually I did. Before I decided to buy it, I asked a friend of mine who works for the city, in the planning department mind you, what they were going to do with that junk yard. He told me they had cited the owner and he had six months to clean it up."

"So, what is it now?"

"It's a large flower garden," Kayla replied, smiling. "That's why I was able to get that loft for well below market value. As a matter of fact, several thousands less than the initial offer. The way I saw it, the developer had made his money ten times over on those lofts. He could well afford to give me that one."

"Sounds nice. So, how's the family? Your dad? Laura?" he glanced at her while he maneuvered the Mercedes into the traffic.

"Dad's wonderful. He retired a couple of years ago, so he's been traveling a lot. He's even dating."

"What? Your dad? Joseph, dating? I thought he would never date."

"I know. So did I. Well, you know, after mom cut out, he didn't seem interested in dating. He had made us his primary focus. But now, he's got so many girlfriends he forgets their names." Kayla winced, then smiled. At first, the idea of her father dating seemed foreign to her, but now she was just happy he was no longer pining over her mother. Dang, Jeanette. She hadn't thought of her return in nearly an hour. Now here she was again — invading her thoughts and causing her mind to spin.

"And Laura?"

"Single. No kids. Lives with dad. And still has one hell of a temper."

"Don't I know it," he responded.

"I don't remember Laura ever turning her venom on you."

"I know you don't," Allen huffed. "I never told you this, but after we broke up your sister cursed me out something fierce. I had no idea she knew such words. Then she stopped by my place, wielding a red Louisville Slugger to make sure she got her point across." He shook his head.

"No!" Kayla's eyes were wide. "She showed up with a baseball bat?!"

"Yup, sure did. So, I got the hint."

Kayla knew her sister could be quite a demon when angered, but she had no idea that she had gone to such lengths to ensure that Allen would never contact her.

"I see you did. Hell, then I really feel for . . . " Kayla stopped. She didn't want to go into how Laura might react when she found out that Jeanette was coming back to stay.

"You feel?" He glanced over at her.

"Huh?"

"You were saying, 'you feel for?' "

She watched the curiosity creep across his face. She started to tell him all about Jeanette, to get off her chest the hurt and anger she felt toward her mother, but she decided against it. Besides, why let him think we're going to be friends. Stuff like this was best left for friends, not for past lovers. "Oh, never mind. Trivial stuff."

"Well, I feel for whoever is going to bear the weight of Laura's wrath. I'd love to meet the joker who's going to come up against that storm and live to tell it," Allen replied.

He fell silent, but Kayla knew it was only momentary. She knew that he was trying to figure out a way to inquire as to what she meant by "trivial stuff."

"So, how are you? Really?" he asked.

"You asked me that already, Allen," Kayla responded a little more tersely than she meant to. Seeing him after all, was beginning to turn out to be both good and bad. Yeah, he still looked good, his aura was still as sexy as she remembered, but the memories were way too bitter to be sweet.

"I mean," Allen recovered. "Is Laura's little sister happily married with a mini tribe?"

"As a matter of fact, no. I'm divorced. No children." Kayla became uneasy. There was a glint in his eye. To her, he seemed relieved, pleased with her response. But she also knew he was playing with her. Yeah, she may have sworn Tim to secrecy, but blood *is* thicker than water. She changed the subject.

"Thanks for the ride. This is really nice of you."

"Don't mention it. I couldn't very well leave you out there wet and shivering, now could I? I can just imagine what Laura would do to me if I had."

Kayla turned her head and watched the cars whizz by as Allen waited at the intersection. The silence surrounded them. She turned back and watched his long fingers, the veins visible in his large hands, as they strummed an imaginary tune on the steering wheel. He was the first to speak.

"How's the teaching thing going?"

Kayla looked up into his face.

"I ran into somebody who told me that," Allen stammered. He knew where he got his information. And he knew Kayla would be angry if she found out. "Umm, I can't remember who it was."

Kayla raised her eyebrows. "We don't know many of the same people, Allen, so I don't know who could have told you." She lied. She knew who it was. She just wanted to see how far Allen would go to shield his brother.

"I don't remember, Kayla," he stated, then looked at her. "But anyway I'm impressed. I really am. I know you had always wanted to teach."

"You have a good memory. I love teaching. It's one of the few things that have gone right over the years," Kayla said, then realized how that must have sounded. She didn't want Allen to think that in ten years her life had not been filled with loving nights and dreamy days. But truths be told, they hadn't.

"You always work on Saturday's?"

"No, I was grading papers. I was so into them that I forgot the time. Then my friend called and we decided to hang out tonight," Kayla ended. No use in letting him know whether the friend was male or female.

"Are you going any place specific?" Allen asked. She watched him study her as he waited for her response while they sat at the traffic light. Kayla turned away just as horns began to blare behind them.

"No, just a little coffee house," she responded, nonchalantly waving her hand in the air.

They continued onward, yet neither spoke. Kayla closed her eyes, but she wasn't the least bit tired. As a matter of fact, she did so to keep from watching him. When the car came to a smooth stop she opened her eyes and sat straight up.

"You're home," Allen whispered.

She looked straight at him sitting near her, one arm set lazily atop the head rest of her seat, his face inches from hers. She batted her eyes and rubbed them absently. The street lamp cast an affectionate glow across the smooth outline of his face, his sensuous smile. She knew this was no dream. She was actually sitting next to Allen Dawson.

"Well, thank you for the ride, Mr. Dawson."

"You're welcome, Ms. Martin. I hope my lack of conversation was not the cause of you falling asleep on me?"

"No, I'm a little tired. Plus this car is way too comfortable. The seats alone make you feel as if you're lying in bed."

Kayla winced at her words and reached for the door handle. "Allen, thanks again for the ride. Take care."

She felt his hand on hers. She turned to see he was struggling to say something. She watched as his mouth opened then shut.

"Yes?" Kayla asked cooly, pulling her hand from his.

He remained silent. Kayla wasn't interested in hearing what he had to say. Sure it was kind of him to give her a ride home, it was actually good seeing him again, but that was enough. She was through with Allen, had been for a long time. She wanted no part of him, this day or any other. "Well, Mr. Dawson, I better get inside. My friend is waiting for me and I'm already late."

"Well, I could wait and give you a lift over," Allen stated, his eyes were hopeful as he stared into her face.

"No, that won't be necessary. Thank you for the offer. I really have to go."

"If you must." Allen reached for her hand again, then pulled back when he noticed she flinched. "It was great bumping into you. You watch those cabbies."

"Tell me about it." Kayla pushed the car door open, took off his coat, retrieved her jacket from the back seat, then turned and faced him. "I would have frozen to death had you not come along. I owe you one."

"Kayla, you never answered my question."

"Which one?" she responded. "I thought I answered all of your questions?"

"Will you have dinner with me?"

"You didn't ask me to have dinner with you."

"Well, I am now. Will you have dinner with me some time?"

"I'll have to see about that. My students keep me pretty busy."

"I see. Well, here's my card. When you get some time, call me. I'd love to continue playing catch up."

"Thanks again, Allen."

Kayla retrieved the rest of her belongings, stepped out of the car, and ran to her building. She looked at his business card, then stuffed it in the folds of her purse. She had no intention of seeing Allen for dinner or anything else for that matter.

Chapter 4

"You won't believe what happened to me." Kayla sighed loudly as she sat down at the table occupied by Amina and some gorgeous brother. Amina widened her expressive hazel eyes, her eyebrows raised, giving Kayla the unspoken code: Just met this one.

"Kayla, this is Gregory. Gregory this is my girl, Kayla."

Kayla accepted Gregory's outstretched hand. She winced slightly. His grip was a little too much like a vice. She rubbed her hand and looked into the brother's face. Yeah, she thought to herself, this brother was fine, with his cafe au lait complexion, pencil thin mustache and connecting beard.

Amina leaned over to Kayla.

"I know this story is going to be a blast," she snickered.

"And you know it is," Kayla agreed, but she wasn't keen on the idea of telling the story in front of a total stranger. She looked into his face again and noticed that his eyebrows met in the center of his forehead. Kayla thought instantly of Ming the Merciless.

"So, tell me why you're over two hours late." Amina tapped her long, red, catlike nails on the table, then turned to Gregory. "Kayla always has good stories. Her life is like a Cecil B. DeMille production. A cast of thousands."

Amina and Gregory laughed. Kayla frowned. She was going to have to talk to Amina about that.

"Please do tell," Gregory's deep, melodic voice boomed. He licked his lips and set his eyes on Kayla's face like glue. "I like a good story."

Kayla raised her right eyebrow. Strike one. This guy was flirting with her. And Amina and Kayla had a firm rule never to hit on the same guy.

"Well, when I left the office, I was out hailing a cab when one came by and splashed water all over me."

"No!" Amina said, her eyes wide. Kayla nodded. "I know you cussed him out, righteous like? You probably had that head moving and those arms waving. Like the robot on Lost in Space. Warning, Warning!" Amina laughed again and touched Gregory on his jacket clad forearm resting on the table.

Kayla finished, ending with how Allen happened along and drove her home. She watched as Amina turned her head and faced her. She knew all about the breakup between her and Allen, as well as the deep pain Kayla had felt as a result of it. Signaling the waitress to their table, Amina ordered a round of flavored coffee and some sandwiches. She tapped Kayla on the shoulder, turned her head so Gregory couldn't read her lips, and mouthed, "We'll talk about this later," then changing the subject, they began discussing the weather, their respective jobs, and just about anything else she could think of besides Allen.

Kayla was grateful. She wasn't inclined to talk about him in front of this total stranger. To prove it, she avoided eye contact and instead scanned the small, cozy coffee house.

Java Oasis had become a place where the thirty plus, and then some, crowd gathered to hear good jazz, mingle and enjoy a wide selection of flavored coffees without the hassle of a less mature crowd. She and Amina had found the spot while heading home from a day of shopping on the Magnificent Mile. And ever since, they had made the coffee house one of their haunts. Nestled between two buildings on south Michigan Avenue, its warm atmosphere, pale yellow walls and outdoor patio tables and matching chairs evoked a feeling of being in the Carribean. Several pieces of black art were arranged fastidiously along the far wall — each piece for sale. One painting in particular always caught her eye. It was Pampered by the popular artist WAK, the artist's initials spelled backwards. The bold, vibrant gold gave way to four brothers, of various hues and body shapes on their knees taking care of four sisters, of the same varying hues. Each time she stepped into the coffee house, her eyes spied the painting, calling forth a fantasy of a man lovingly caressing her. How she would like for some brother to pamper her from head to toe.

Kayla was in her normal fantasy when Gregory interrupted. "Did you get the guy's number?" She grimaced, then rolled her eyes upward. Damn, he had successfully brought the conversation back around to Allen.

"Umm, Dear," Amina patted him on his hand. "We're not going to discuss it."

"He gave me his business card," Kayla responded before she knew it.

"And you're going to call him, right?" Gregory asked.

Amina looked over at Kayla with a questioning look in her best friend's face. And though she didn't utter a word, she knew that Amina would want to know why she wouldn't call Allen. Kayla pursed her lips, then smiled demurely, refusing to answer his question. They were relieved when Gregory excused himself and headed to the bathroom.

"Where on earth did you pick him up?" Kayla inquired the minute he was out of hearing range.

"You know this is our table," Amina chuckled. "He was sitting here when I arrived. And you know me. I never turn down the opportunity to sit with a handsome man."

The pair laughed.

"Anyway, so, Mr. Allen Dawson gave you a ride home, then gave you his card. Are you going to call him?"

"Girl, I'm not sure." She frowned. "There's a lot of bad blood between us."

"It's been ten years. A lot happens and changes in ten years. Why not call and see what he has to say?" Amina tapped Kayla's hands resting on the table.

"I may, but . . ." Kayla was interrupted when Amina shifted in her seat.

"Well, well, look what the cat done drug in," she said snidely. "It's Kayla's dream date."

"How are you ladies tonight?" Myles stopped at their table. Kayla watched his exaggerated motions as he took Amina's hand in his, bent slightly, then kissed the back of it. Amina snatched her hand away and wiped it on a napkin.

"Oh, come now Ms. Amina. You shouldn't be like that."

"I'm trying to avoid the plague," she replied, then tossed the napkin on the tray of a passing waitress. Kayla couldn't help laughing. Myles had been another of her dates from hell, which for the past year was all she seemed to have attracted. If it wasn't the game players, it was the heart breakers. The game players she could deal with, but the heart breakers were another story. Myles was in the former category; he was definitely a game player. She had met him one month after she and Amina had become regulars at Java Oasis. Slight in build and sporting a neatly trimmed goatee, his smooth, flawless, creamy chocolate skin, and eyes that matched, made him look much younger than his forty-five years. Kayla didn't consider him fine or cute, but she had been attracted to what she thought was his confidence.

In the beginning he was charming, but his charm soon gave way to agitation. The more she got to know Myles, the less she liked him.

"Right. Whatever." He dismissed Amina and turned his attention to Kayla. "So, Kayla." Myles kissed her on the cheek. "Why haven't I heard from you? I thought we were going to brunch last Sunday?"

"Was that last Sunday?" Kayla placed her slender fingers across her chest and fluttered her long eye lashes. "Oh, my, time sure flies."

"Well, what's the excuse this time?" Myles pulled a chair from another table and forcing it between Kayla and Amina, he sat down. "You, don't mind?" Myles didn't wait for a response. "Anyway, I waited for you to call."

"Sure Myles, and I'm a millionaire." Kayla rolled her eyes. "I told you that I wasn't going, but for some inexplicable reason you won't take 'no' for an answer."

"Call me persistent. I get what I want."

Amina looked at Kayla. "Dang, I thought slavery ended a long time ago."

Myles persisted. "Kayla, can we go outside and talk?"

"No, Myles, its cold outside. Say whatever you have to here."

"Okay." Myles breathed out heavily. "I know what I said was brash of me. But I didn't know any other way. You won't listen. I'm the one for you and you know it. But, if it helps any, I'm sorry."

"Yeah, a sorry mother . . . "

"Amina!" Kayla stared open mouthed at her.

"My deepest apologies," Amina said sarcastically. "Continue on. With your sorry ass." Amina ended and held up two fingers in a sign of peace.

"Finish, Myles." Kayla sighed.

"Thank you, Heckle." He sneered at Amina.

"Heckle?" Amina stood and placed both of her hands on the edges of the small table, then leaned close to Myles, her nose inches from his face. "Why you sawed off, no class, raggedy, ghetto . . ."

Kayla then stood, ending the beginning of yet another verbal battle between Amina and Myles. There was definitely no love between the two, and Kayla knew that if he were to be heard out, she would have to go outside with him. "Come on Myles." Kayla tapped him on his shoulder, then exited the coffee house.

The cold night air swirled around her as she pulled her fur jacket up around her neck and her beret down around her ears. She watched Myles's breath escape his mouth and disappear up into the night. She knew his impetuous and overly self-centered manner had caused her to rethink ever going out with him again. His attitude left her wanting to scream.

"I know that stuff I was talking last week was crazy, 'bout you needing a man and all that other crap 'bout changing for me, but what do you say to a woman who leaves you spellbound?" Myles asked.

Kayla began to walk away. Myles fell in step beside her. "Myles, you shouldn't tell anyone that kind of trash. All that garbage about you having a program for me. That you can teach me things, like I'm some young school girl. That's more than a bit presumptuous of you."

"I know. It was dumb. I was at a loss of words."

"So, your answer is to verbally spar with me, almost like you do with Amina, even though you and I both know it's futile. Yet, you insist on going toe to toe with us. I don't get it, Myles. I'm not looking to indulge your ego by continually engaging in a war of words or wits with you. I don't think, no, I do not want to have to continually show my self worth to you. I strive for peace in my life. Not constant turmoil."

"Kayla, I understand your point, but you're arrogant. You know that? And who says I want you to prove how smart you are?"

"First off, Myles, I'm secure not arrogant. There's a big difference in case you didn't know. And second, when you continually challenge me, the things I say, its like I've got to be on. I can't stand it. Anyway, why are we talking about this? I ran into your girlfriend the other night when I was here. She let it be known to anyone who would listen that you two have been spending a lot of time together."

"Who? Peggy?"

"Yeah." Kayla smiled.

"We're nothing but friends. I have a lot of female friends." Myles defended. They stopped at the corner. "Wait. Is that what this is all about?"

"No, but to be honest, Myles, I don't like the way you come across. You act as though you are the gift to all women, when in fact, you are a gift to your momma and no one else. This world does rotate without you, you know?"

"Damn, Kayla, you cold. Whatever brother broke your heart, broke it well."

"Myles, that has nothing to do with it," Kayla's voice rose higher than she wanted it. True, Myles had hit a nerve. No, she hadn't found that special one. And true, her heart had been broken — ten years ago in fact. But still, all of that is past. She wasn't going to let Myles get the best of her. She was through being nice to him. "Tell me, Myles, why is it when you men get caught in the game, you have to try and flip the script and make it the woman's fault?"

"No flippancy here. I think what I said is true."

Kayla turned and headed back to the coffee house. She could hear Myles's footsteps coming close.

"Wait, Kayla. Let's start over. I like you a lot. Can we start over?"

"As friends."

"What if I don't want to be just your friend?" Myles stopped her and looked into her eyes. "Then what?"

"Then we won't be anything," Kayla replied. Her tone spoke her true feelings — not a hint of emotion. She watched intently as Myles stared at her. She liked what she saw. He was stunned — didn't know what move to make next.

Kayla shrugged her shoulders and turned her back. She heard his foot steps as he walked to his car, got in and drove off.

"Where's the weasel?" Amina joked as Kayla took her seat at the table.

"You ain't nothing nice," she replied, then rolled her eyes.

"He gets on my nerves. He just rubs me the wrong way. Has from the moment we met him. Thinking he's all that.

Humph! That crap is old, especially for a man his age. What is he, damn near fifty?"

"He's forty-five."

"Close enough."

Kayla changed the subject. "Where's Gregory?"

"He got paged and left, which is fine with me." Amina dismissed him with a wave of her hand. "See that cutie over there?" She nodded her head to the right. Kayla glanced over at a brother sitting two tables away. "One's out to lunch, so I guess he's over for dinner?"

Kayla laughed at Amina's phrase, then settled back to listen as the final set began. The jazz quartet moved effortlessly from playing famous tunes of John Coltrane to Joe Sample. Their heads nodded and bopped in sync with the music, and Amina occasionally closed her eyes when the saxophone player belted out a long, melodious tune.

At the end of the final set they got up to leave. Kayla waited nearby, watching Amina smile gaily at her next suitor, flirting shamelessly; then she pulled out a pen and piece of paper, scribbled something, and handed it over. Waving her hand and walking slowly away, she allowed her hips to sway just enough. Kayla snickered. Amina was something else when it came to men. She could easily take them or leave them, and it was this attitude that kept them calling her.

"Let's get outta here?" Amina hailed a cab, gave the driver their respective addresses, and settled into her seat. She was silent for several blocks before she spoke. "You need to call him, Kayla. Get out the things that you wanted to say, but didn't. If nothing else, you may get some surprising answers. You never know."

Kayla laid her head back in thought. She wasn't sure about calling Allen, but then again, she might finally get what she wanted — an answer to why he broke off their relationship so suddenly.

Chapter 5

Allen's mind twirled. He let her go once. He wasn't about to make the same mistake twice.

He had watched Kayla disappear through the double glass doors of her loft, then around a large support beam. In all his business dealings, day in and day out, negotiating and securing multimillion dollar contracts, he was tongue-tied when it came to persuading her to stay a while longer. Allen had to admit that he truly missed her. In the ten years they had been apart, he hadn't met a woman quite like her, one as vivacious, yet independent as Kayla.

He was pleased to see she hadn't changed. A little feistier maybe, but he sensed she had the same sweet, loving nature he had liked about her. And he felt the charge, the tension between them — had felt her presence as she sat near him. He wanted to touch her, to let his fingers trace the familiar outline of her smooth face, yet he knew better, for the silence they shared only stood as a stark reminder of how hurt she had been when he broke up with her.

Allen knew from the blank look in her eyes that she was finished talking to him. He was resigned to let it go, for now, but there was no way he would ever let her out of his life again. He vowed to do whatever he had to, to make sure she would be in his life for good.

"Oh, yes, Kayla, you will see me again," Allen promised.

It was well past two in the morning when Kayla finally climbed into her bed. Her head ached as she ran down the events of the past twenty-four hours. Jeanette was returning to Chicago, and she had run into Allen for the first time in ten years. His face slipped into her mind. She had often wondered what he was up to, how he was doing, but had resisted asking his brother Tim about him.

Kayla stepped out of bed, turned on the lamp and grabbed her purse. She fished out the business card and read it. Dawson Design, Inc., Allen Dawson, President. She was impressed — Allen had said he was going to own his own company one day.

She placed the card back in her purse, turned off the light, returned to bed, and fell into a fitful sleep.

Allen pulled slowly into his driveway. He let his eyes sweep across the large, handsome house he had spent the last three years refurbishing. Luck seemed to be with him. His business contracts had increased substantially, he got his dream car for a "hell of a deal," and paid pennies on the dollar for his home, an old three-story greystone in an area that was termed as 'up and coming.' When he first saw the house, it's gray brick turned green from mold, he knew it held a lot of potential.

For several months, Allen lived in the house while he refurbished it, glad that it was summer and not winter — the heating system was completely shot. But more important, the house gave him something to occupy his time, other than the disturbing thoughts that resulted from his recurring nightmare — a screaming child and the back of a woman. To compound his nightmare, were the continued failed attempts at a solid relationship. Yeah, he felt he had been lucky in everything but relationships; this he regretted. Not to the point where he wouldn't date, but to an extent where he just could not commit. His buddies would laugh at him for not being able to hold on to a date longer than three months and they had begun placing bets on how long the latest woman would last. He stared at the house and remembered the last conversation he and his childhood buddy, Mike, had concerning his love life.

"So, is Sharon in or out?" Mike had joked while he sipped a beer. "Brother, you've got some track record."

"Hey, man, you know it ain't like that," Allen replied, trying to sound nonchalant. "She and I just didn't jive. You know?"

"I thought she was cool. You should have let me hit on her. I saw her first."

Allen laughed at Mike. "You're married! Remember? Want another beer?"

"I know. And you know I have no intention of cheating. And yeah, get me another beer."

When Allen returned, Mike continued. "Man, and you're a successful architect. You've got this large, phat house with no one in it but you and little man. And you're damned near forty and still no woman to speak of."

"I'm thirty-seven," Allen replied.

"Whatever," Mike dismissed.

Allen watched him. He appreciated the concern his friend was showing, but he was not in the mood for dredging up old wounds. "So? And when the right woman comes along I'll know it."

"Not at the rate you're going. I know what you're doing, Allen, my man. You waiting for a clone of Kayla."

"Yeah right," Allen barked. "You don't know what you're talking about. That was a long time ago."

"And in that time you have had more failed dates than either of us wants to mention. Like that sister, what was her name? You know the one, the HR consultant? Come on Allen, you know her name."

"Keshia," Allen mumbled.

"That's right." Mike snapped his fingers. "Keshia. That's her name. Now she was some sister. Had all the right stuff. She was independent. Made money. Had no dependents. Her own place. She was all that."

"But she was no bag of chips. She had her own issues. Serious ones at that."

"And like you don't?" Mike laughed before turning serious. "Man, but I know you were crazy about Kayla. Then y'all broke up and then you married Donna. What, some six months after you and Kayla broke up? Now, I'm going to go out on a limb here, cause I'm your boy and I loves ya, but Allen, when you love someone you got to show it. You didn't love Donna and she bent over backwards to try and make you love her."

"You can't make a person love you," Allen replied angrily, shifting his weight uneasily on the large black leather sofa. He didn't want to discuss his ex-wife, Donna.

"And so Donna paid for your ghosts. Besides, you didn't show it to Kayla either. But I know you didn't love Donna, and I know you loved Kayla."

"How do you know that, Einstein?"

"How do I know what? That you didn't love Donna or that you were in love with Kayla?"

"Both."

"As for Donna, if you had loved her, you wouldn't have let her walk like she did. Leaving you alone to raise Daniel with no forwarding address to be had. Donna was crazy about you, but a woman can't compete with a ghost and competing with Kayla's ghost is a monster."

"Donna shouldn't have tried to compete with Kayla."

"Did she have a choice?" He looked Allen squarely in the eye. "And that brings me to Kayla. You wanted Kayla. You loved her. We all saw it, but you couldn't bring yourself to admit it. To commit to it. I mean, did you ever try to explain your true feelings to Kayla? That you were afraid of true love? That you didn't believe that what she had to offer was real? Did you even try?"

"We were young."

"And so that makes it okay? You weren't that young. Man, you letting life pass you by."

"Oh, so now that you're married and got what you consider the perfect woman, you're an expert?" Allen got up from the couch.

"Man, I know a good woman when I spot her," he retorted quickly as he watched Allen fumble with the television remote. "Donna was good, but she was no Kayla."

"You got that right." Allen slumped back down on the couch

"What you say?"

He shrugged his shoulders. "Never mind."

The pair fell silent. Allen stared at the television, images of Kayla's smile roaming through his head. Frankly, he didn't know how to make it right. How to tell her he had loved her more than life itself. Besides, that mean sister of hers vowed to kill him if he came within ten inches of her. But he knew that was just an excuse.

"Allen, I know you don't like folks in your business. I can understand that. But you have got to either get over Kayla or make it right with her. It's been too long."

"You don't understand," Allen said, his voice low.

"Try me." Mike challenged.

"You've been listening to Vanzant too much, Bro."

"And you should listen to her. The things she says about brothers and our fears are real."

"Oh, you trippin', man." Allen chided, his voice tinged in anger.

"And you're lonely," Mike barked back. "Anyway, I tried. You defend it if you want to. But you either find Kayla, make it work, or get over it. There ain't another woman like her, and until you get that into your thick head you are forever going to search for her. And no two exist. End of speech."

"Good. I was beginning to wonder about you, Mike."

"Anyway, where's little man?"

"He's with Tim. They went to some new play joint. Odyssey Fun Place, or something like that."

Allen had to smile. His son, Daniel, was the one good thing that came from his and Donna's short-lived marriage. Donna had become pregnant right after they married, and though Allen wasn't ready to be a father, he accepted the inevitable. And when Daniel was born, he was in love — unconditionally. Six months after Donna gave birth she disappeared, leaving only a letter which explained how she had tried to love him, give him love, but he wouldn't, couldn't, reciprocate.

For months after Donna had disappeared, Allen read the letter every day, trying to understand — to sort out his own feelings. He could not forgive her for leaving him to raise Daniel alone, so much so that after two years of no contact, he had her parental rights revoked. But, as the years passed, he came to understand more and more why she had left. Mike had been right. Donna knew he would never love her, and hadn't loved her when they married.

His mind came back to the present. On his way home from one of his construction sites, he spied the rain-soaked Kayla. And for the first time since their chance meeting he laughed aloud at the scene. Actually, he saw her first, when she whirled out of the university's building. He had known where she was. Had her phone number. Knew all about her ex-husband, Jonathan. But the fear of rejection kept him silent. In fact, he could think of no reason why she wouldn't reject him. I was some piece of work back then. When he saw her, he knew he had to seize the moment and try and make it right with her.

He shrugged his shoulders. After ten years, he thought, the memories wouldn't be so fresh and up close. True, he had been wrong, he reasoned as he pushed the automatic garage door opener. He knew he owed her much more than she got.

Allen stepped out of his car and walked around to the passenger side, visualizing Kayla sitting there, her body language conveying her uneasiness at being with him. He sighed, grabbed his brief case and began to shut the door. A glimmer on the floor of the car caught his eye and he reached for the object. Allen held up a gold bracelet with the four charms attached to it and smiled, remembering that Kayla had been wearing it.

"Now, she has no choice but to meet me again."

Chapter 6

"So, Linda, how's it going?" Kayla peered around the door jam of the small office. She liked the new receptionist. Liked her style. Linda Raynor. The name fit, Kayla thought as she gazed at Linda's short curly hair colored a bronze blonde. No more than fifty, Kayla observed how the style and color of Linda's hair perfectly complemented her pear shaped, golden graham-cracker colored face. Even her light brown eyes held a warmth that Kayla liked and was immediately drawn to.

"So far so good, Professor Martin," Linda replied, the smile on her face shone through her eyes.

"Good. Now, don't hesitate to call on me if you need something. I'm available if you need me."

"Thank you, Professor Martin."

"Linda," she began, her arched eyebrows raised. "If you want to continue to work here, you're going to have to call me Kayla. Everyone else does, even the students." She smiled.

"Okay, Miss Kayla," she replied, her light voice cracked. "How's that?"

"Well, Miss Raynor," she smiled, a playful sarcasm in her voice. "I'm not too fond of Miss Kayla either."

"Okay, how about we strike a deal?" Linda tilted her head to the right. "You call me Linda and I'll call you Kayla. How's that?"

"Sounds good, cause calling me by any other name will most certainly get you out the front door." They both laughed. Kayla's mirth tapered. "Allow me to let you get back to work, but remember, do not hesitate to ask if you need anything."

"Thanks, Kayla." Linda smiled. "I think I'm going to like it here."

Kayla tapped her neatly manicured nails on top of the plain wooden desk, waved her hand over her head and continued to her small office located on the top floor of the university's main building. Her office sported a wonderful view of Buckingham Fountain and Lake Michigan. She sat at her desk and thought about Jonathan and how they had met. Looking back, Kayla could see that Jonathan was just like her — searching for someone to ease the pain and despair that followed a broken heart.

When they met at the annual faculty Christmas party, Kayla was attracted to him immediately. A friend of one of the faculty members, Jonathan's smooth, bronze-colored skin was accentuated by his odd colored eyes, light brown mixed with specks of green. She had never seen eyes like his, and they drooped, giving him a sleepy, sexy look. Kayla thought of them as bedroom eyes. And he was tall, at least six feet-four inches, with a slight build. His jet black hair was neatly cut close on the sides and connected to a precisely cut beard. When they spoke, he stared intently into her eyes. As the evening wore on, she felt the voice, deep inside her telling her to tread carefully, but she ignored that voice and let her loneliness become her guide.

After just six months of dating, Jonathan proposed and she accepted, once again ignoring her gut instincts that told her what she was doing was all wrong. The attention he provided was what she had felt she needed, even craved, after her breakup with Allen.

Why didn't I want to listen? Kayla asked herself as she absently flipped through the pages of her lesson plan for her upcoming class. Why didn't I listen to my mind instead of my heart?

"This is all Allen's fault." Kayla pounded her fist on the desk. "If I had been in my right mind, I would've known that I was on the serious rebound."

Linda's voice interrupted her self admonishment. "Kayla, your sister, Laura, is on line one." Kayla liked the professionalism the receptionist displayed. She had hoped Linda wouldn't turn out the way the last one did — not picking up the phone by the second ring and letting mail and class documents pile up on her desk.

Kayla picked up the receiver. "Hey Sis, what's up?" She thought of her big sister, then their mother. Laura was built just like Jeanette, a small waist, wide hips, and a full bosom. She even wore her reddish-brown hair like their mother had — in loose ringlet curls which cascaded about her round face and perfectly complemented her chestnut colored eyes.

"Enjoying the weather. Hey, that girl's pretty sharp," Laura began. "You got her screening calls already?"

"You know it's necessary. How's North Carolina today?"

"North Carolina is wonderful. Hot. Brian and I are having a ball. We've laid out on this beach for three days straight. I'm at least two shades darker."

"I bet. From the looks of the post card it seems like heaven." Kayla wished she had a steady beau like Laura, who never seemed to have to try hard to attract a date.

"Yeah, it is. You should have come with us. The time away would have done you some good."

"You know I couldn't. We're coming up on midterms. But I'll make up for it this summer, when we hit Jamaica."

"Wait! Back up. What do you mean 'it's necessary'?" Laura asked.

"Well, Jonathan's been calling again." Kayla responded, then felt a tinge of guilt. She wasn't being forthright. He'd been calling, but she hadn't done a thing to discourage it.

"What?" Laura screamed into the phone. "You've got to be joking, Kayla! After all he's done, cheating and having that kid, you still talk to him?"

"Well, no." Kayla didn't know how to get out of this one. She silently wished she hadn't mentioned it at all. In some crazed way, Jonathan's calls seemed to entertain her, made her feel wanted. Kayla knew it was all bordering on insanity, but Jonathan's calls provided some sort of primal relief from the lack of a real relationship, no matter how temporary the retreat was. Besides, what harm was it? She didn't go out with him. She simply accepted his calls at home and at work.

"Girl, you need your head examined," Laura chided. "When is he going to get a clue and move on? He got what he wanted, that hussy, Serena. Now, it's time for him to accept it and move on."

"He and Serena broke up," Kayla replied.

"And so now he wants to come slithering back. Umph, girl, I don't want to talk about it anymore. You need to get straight, is all I'm gonna say. How's Dad?"

"Fine. We had lunch on Saturday, then I went into the office to grade some papers, met Amina at the coffee house, and that's it." Kayla left out the news about running into Allen, as well as their mother's impending return. She had resolved to wait for a perfect time to tell her. With Laura, though, when it came to Jeanette, there might never be a perfect time. She nervously fingered her wrist. She couldn't fathom where she had placed her gold charm bracelet. The last time she wore it was the day she ran into Allen. She gasped.

"What's the matter?" Laura asked.

"Nothing."

Linda's voice interrupted the beginnings of what Kayla knew would be an inquisition. "Kayla, you have a call on line two."

She was happy for the diversion. "You heard?"

"Yeah, another call. Better you than me. I'll be back on Saturday. I'll see you then. And Kayla?"

"Yes, Laura?"

"You need to end this game you're playing with Jonathan. I'm serious. I don't want to see you hurt again. Don't make me have to give that man a straight up Southside, kick your butt into a sewer hole, fight!"

Kayla chuckled at her sister's threat. "Got cha, Laura. Hang up."

"I am. I can't believe any of this," Laura said, then began to laugh.

"What's so funny?"

"I'm sitting here watching Brian make faces at me. He's in the water. If only Jonathan were there, Brain could drown him. No more problems."

"Oh, that's bad," Kayla chortled nervously. "I gotta run. Tell Brian I said hello."

"I'll do that. Talk to you later."

"All right, Laura."

"Bye, Kayla. I love you."

"I love you, too."

Kayla pressed the flashing light. "This is Kayla Martin," she responded into the receiver. No one responded. "Hello," she repeated. In the distance, she could hear the sounds of traffic just before the line went dead.

She left her office and went to Linda.

"There was no one there, do you know who it was?"

"It was some lady, said she was a student. She asked for you by name."

"Umm, that's odd. There was no one on the line when I picked up." Kayla tapped her slender fingers on the desk. "Oh, well, if its important, she'll call back." Kayla began to walk away.

"Oh, Kayla, an Allen Dawson called today."

Kayla spun on her heels and ordered her emotions to still. "Did he say what he wanted?"

"No," Linda answered. "And he's called several times."

Kayla eyed Linda. If he had called before, why was she just now getting the messages? As if reading her mind, Linda responded.

"He didn't want to leave a message the first three times he called. But I memorized his voice. Kinda soft. Warm. The fourth time he called I made him leave a message."

"Thanks, I wonder what he wants?" Kayla asked. "Did he leave a number?" Linda handed over a message slip.

"Must be really important to call four times." She raised her eyebrows, a knowing smile on her face. "Real important." She repeated.

Kayla could see the curiosity in her eyes and ignored it. Instead, she mumbled a thanks, then reached out to retrieve the number. The last thing she wanted to do was discuss Allen with the new receptionist. She placed the slip of paper in her blazer pocket and went to her first class of the day. As she proceeded with her lesson plan, interacting with her students, thoughts of Jonathan and Allen intruded into her discussion. She knew she was playing with Jonathan, giving him hope every time she spoke with him. It was time for her to stop. Time to truly move on. So what that she was alone. It was her choice and she had to stand by it no matter how miserable she felt some days. Letting Jonathan call her only served to make matters worse, especially if she should meet someone special. Someone special, she repeated. Allen's smiling face and sensuous eyes came to her. In that instant, she knew she had been putting off the inevitable. For ten years she had wondered, even lost sleep over why they broke up in the first place. Kayla knew that her running into Allen was no fluke. To her, nothing was ever by chance — everything had a reason.

It was time. Time she called him and just outright ask him what the hell had been on his mind back then. Why had he treated her so coldly? Her next thought caused her to cringe. Was she truly prepared for his response? Could she handle it if he told her that he truly hadn't loved her? She wrestled with those thoughts for several moments, then came to a resolve. Closure. Her relationship with Allen was the one situation in her life that had no resolution — remained unfinished. She made up her mind. She was going to call Allen Dawson.

Chapter 7

Allen sat at the wide, white Formica drafting table with his back to the door. He studied his recent drawings of a cultural center to be built on the South Side of Chicago in the Bronzeville community. The drawings, which he completed by hand, were intricate in detail, each line meticulously drawn to show the beauty of the proposed building. He would spare no expense for this project and had decided to personally oversee the project from start to finish.

The site of the center, on the corner of 35th Street and King Drive, had at one time been the home of the first black-owned insurance company in Chicago. And like many buildings in that area, the site had fallen into a state of disrepair and continued neglect. Allen knew the project was a golden opportunity to combine its rich history with the future, not to mention that a project of this magnitude would solidify his position as one of the top black architects in Chicago. Maybe even across the nation.

His firm had outbid several architectural giants across the city, and even though the bidding process had been long and tedious, Allen knew he couldn't be beat. He had hired some of the best black architects in the country, and they in return repaid him by working long hours and putting their hearts into his vision.

Allen rubbed his eyes with the back of his hand, then glanced over at the black lacquer clock on the wall.

"Why hasn't she called me back?" he wondered aloud as he picked up Kayla's charm bracelet from the table. He had left several messages at her office.

He stood, stretched his broad frame, and walked to the window which overlooked the bustling activity of 87th Street on the South Side of Chicago. From this view he could see the various street hawkers with their collars pulled up around their ears to protect them from the city's biting cold wind. He held the bracelet up to the window and closely examined the four charms hanging from it. One charm was in the shape of a cat. The others were the shape of a star, an initial in its center. One had an "L" on it, so Allen guessed it stood for her sister, Laura; another, the letter "K," he guessed stood for Kayla, followed by the letter "J."

"It's got to stand for Joseph, her father." He hoped, wanting to believe that the initial didn't belong to her ex husband. "Surely she's not still carrying a torch for that fool."

He knew all about Kayla's relationship with Jonathan from Tim. So much for payoffs. Tim, his older brother by four years, was never good at keeping secrets. He had told Allen all about their little mechanical arrangements nearly five years ago. And since then, Allen had tracked her life through Tim and Amina. If Kayla knew that her best friend Amina had been dating Tim on and off for over a year, she would die, for it was because of Amina's pillow talk that Tim was able to give him a ringside view of Kayla's love life. Allen knew, when Tim revealed that Kayla wasn't involved with anyone, that it was time for him to contact her.

When he had to check on the construction of his latest project, the Wright Theater in the new theater district downtown, it gave him the perfect excuse, the absolute perfect opportunity to be within walking distance of Kayla's office. After two weeks of walking past her building, he had finally run into her. Allen had said a silent prayer to God — thanking him for the once in a lifetime opportunity.

"She's through with Jonathan for sure, but this Myles guy has got to go." He laughed at his sudden feelings of jealousy. "Well, I did give her up. But not this time."

Allen continued to finger the bracelet before he slipped it back into the pocket of his charcoal gray wool gabardine slacks. He adjusted his deep wine suspenders and straightened his matching tie as he returned to his large mahogany desk near the window. He set his attention to his right and began to study the small replica sitting on a cherrywood display stand.

The replica was the first building he designed. The small statue was re-created in exact detail, from the large stained-glass windows that allowed sun to shine in from all angles, to the inside of the design that boasted ornate wood work which surrounded the sanctuary. Allen had been proudest of that design, a nondenominational church in Atlanta. Every once in a while, he would turn to BET to see his creation. The minister had gone on to build one of the largest black congregations in the nation.

Yet, the project held a bitter memory. It reminded him of his ex-wife, Donna. She had walked out on him and Daniel when he was in Atlanta overseeing the final phase of the project.

The loud intercom interrupted his thoughts. "Mr. Dawson, your brother is here."

Allen sighed. "Thank you, Mrs. Green. Please let him in."

"My main man, what's going' on?" Tim sang, as he strolled through the door.

Allen looked at his older and only brother and laughed. With the exception of their eyes, they looked a lot alike, so much so that people often mistook one for the other. He enjoyed his brother's wide smile as he stood to greet him. They were the only two males in a family of four girls.

"Nothing much. What's up with you?" Allen clasped Tim's hand, then pulled him into a tight hug.

"You know, nothing but the rent," Tim replied, then settled down in a chair across from Allen's desk.

He watched Tim's eyes as they swept back and forth across the office. Allen knew his brother was proud of him, but he always wished that Tim would go into business for himself. A skilled mechanic, he could fix a car better than any mechanic he had ever met. But something inside of him kept him from reaching for that dream.

"Okay, what gives today?" Allen eyed Tim. He prayed he wasn't there for another loan. Every loan turned into a barter — Tim would repair something of Allen's in return for the debt being forgiven.

"Naw, I'm straight today." Tim cut him off. "This weather has been very good for business." He smiled. His even white teeth mixed with his golden light brown eyes gave him an innocent appearance against his deep mocha brown skin.

"Glad to hear it. I don't need a tune up today."

The brothers laughed.

"Amina told me you ran into Kayla." Tim eyed his baby brother.

"Yeah, I did. Damn, news travels fast." Allen raised his eyebrows.

"Yes, it does. I also hear you asked her out to dinner. Did she accept?"

"No, not yet," Allen looked at his hands.

"Well, the field is clear." Tim smiled smugly, stretched his long legs out in front of him, then placed his hands behind his head. "Go for it. The two of you shouldn't have broken up in the first place. I know for a fact that you loved that woman. Otherwise, you wouldn't be so interested in who she's seeing or what she's doing."

Allen sat quietly and began to wonder how this conversation had turned so quickly over to his feelings for Kayla. For the second time in less than a month he had to hear about how much he loved Kayla. First Mike, now Tim.

"When are you fixing her car again?"

"I just tuned it up last month, so it will be a while. But, Allen, you don't need me spying for you any more, and besides Kayla would murder us all if she knew that we were telling her business. I'm out of it. Now the rest is up to you."

He stood and walked over to the window. If he knew Allen, he was finished talking about Kayla and was ready to act. Tim was glad. Their love for each other would either be extinguished or turned up to a full blaze. He returned to the chair and changed the subject. "What are you and little man doing tonight?"

"He wants to go to the show." Allen was glad for the diversion.

"Which one? That new Disney movie?"

Allen laughed. "Don't you know it. Those folks know how to make money. Five dollars for the kid and seven seventy-five for me. And let's not forget the popcorn, soda and candy. Then, as always, little man falls asleep, wakes up when the show is over and has to go to the bathroom. There goes forty bucks down the drain, literally." The brother's laughter was interrupted by the secretary's voice on the phone intercom.

"Yes, Mrs. Green."

"Sir, you have a call on line two. It's a Ms. Martin."

Tim stood quickly and quietly walked toward the door. He mouthed "good-bye," then left, shutting the door behind him.

"Do you ever sit at your desk?"

"Yes, and I return phone calls from those who leave messages. Linda said she had to wrangle one out of you after the fourth call. What's so important?"

"A lot. But seeing you this weekend could be a start."

"Oh, I don't think I like the sound of that."

"It's all good, Kayla. Besides, I think I have something you want."

"Really now? What do you have that you think I may want?"

"I'm going to ignore that question and save it for another day. I have your bracelet."

"Where did you find it? I've been wondering where I lost it. I turned my whole loft upside down."

"It was on the floor of my car. It must have slipped off your wrist. I've been calling you to tell you I found it. You want it back, don't you?"

"Of course I do. When can we meet? I've been missing that bracelet. I'm really glad you have it. I thought either Patton had eaten it or I had lost it."

"Patton?"

"My cat." Kayla laughed. "She eats anything that falls to the floor."

"Never fear. I have it. But, now lets see. Ummm, you're going to have to meet me for dinner to get it back."

"Dinner, ugh?"

"Yup. And in this case, no is not an option."

Silence. Allen didn't like silence. He knew that as long as he could keep her talking she wouldn't have a chance to change her mind. "It's just dinner Kayla. I won't bite you. Besides it will give us a chance to finish our conversation. You know? Play catch up."

"Oh, really? Catch up on what? I teach and I've written a book. That's all."

Allen chuckled. "I know that in between all of that, there have been other interesting things happening in your life," he replied. He hoped his words hadn't let on. "So, how about it? It's the only way you're going to get this bracelet back."

"Then if that's the case, I guess I have no choice. When and where?" she asked, sighing loudly.

"Dang, don't sound so happy about it," Allen replied.

Kayla laughed. "I'll be more than happy to meet you Allen. I want my bracelet back."

"Touche'!" he said and laughed. "Friday, at seven. I'll pick you up."

"All right I'll see you then."

"See you then."

Chapter 8

"Daddy, why you getting all dressed up?" Allen's son, Daniel, asked as he sat on his father's bed and watched him meticulously sift through shirts and slacks. "You got a date tonight?"

Allen stopped and looked at his son through the reflection in the mirror. He turned and sat down on the bed next to Daniel.

"Yes, you can call it that." Allen brushed his hand across his son's closely cropped hair. "I'm meeting an old friend for dinner."

"Is she pretty?"

"How do you know it's a female?"

"'Cause you only get dressed like this for work and for females. And it's dark outside, so you're not going to work."

Allen laughed at his son's observation.

"Now daddy, is she pretty?"

"I think she is, why?" Allen smiled.

"Uncle Tim says you should always date pretty women."

"Oh, really, and what else did your dear old Uncle Tim say?" Allen raised his eyebrows and took a deep breath. He steeled himself. He knew anything Tim had to say could only border on sexist.

"Uncle Tim also said that you should find a good woman and love her."

"You should or I should?"

Daniel giggled. "Daddy, you know I'm too young. I'm only eight. Well, eight going on nine."

"That you are little man." Allen let out a long sigh of relief. "Why don't you go to your room and get the games you want to play with tonight? Your Aunt Yolanda should be here any minute."

"She's going to hang out with me tonight?" Daniel asked before sliding off the bed.

Allen laughed. Lately Daniel didn't like the word babysitter. "Yeah. Did you want to go to Grandma's or hang out with Uncle Tim?"

"No, Auntie's the bomb at Crash Bandi Coot." Daniel smiled, jumped off the bed and ran toward his room.

"Hey, no running." Allen stood and walked back over to the mirror.

"Yes sir," Daniel called back. "Oh, Daddy?"

"Yes, little man, what is it?"

Daniel reappeared in the doorway. "If she's pretty, are you going to let her stick around?"

Allen froze in his place. Up until now, he hadn't thought of the numerous women he had dated as having an effect, if any, on Daniel. For the most part, he had made sure he didn't bring women to the house unless he was serious, and he had only considered getting serious with Sharon and Keshia.

"Come here, Daniel."

"Daddy, did I say something wrong to them?" Daniel's bushy jet black eyebrows crowded his eyes. Allen watched his son walk slowly toward him then stopped to stand in front of him. He watched as Daniel circled the carpet with his foot.

"Daniel, look at me," he began as he sat on the edge of the bed. He gently pulled his son's face upward so that he could look him in the eye. He thought of how much he loved and needed Daniel. "You have done nothing wrong."

"Then why they keep leaving? I liked Sharon."

"What about Keisha?"

"Oh, she was okay, I guess. But she had some really spooky eyes."

"Spooky?"

"Yeah, spooky. Like she had something to hide."

"Umm, and what was it about Sharon that you liked."

"She was pretty and she was good at PlayStation."

Allen laughed and hugged his son closely. Daniel pulled back. "Why did they leave, Daddy?"

Allen rubbed his own face then raked his hand over his son's head.

"Well, Daniel, it's hard to explain." He could see that an explanation was in order. He wanted to be honest with his son, be the one that he could come to, no matter what. "Okay, here it is."

"The truth?" Daniel queried.

"The truth." Allen wasn't quite ready to explain to Daniel the difficulties of relationships, as well as his own fears and how those fears had kept him from committing to either woman. But he decided to throw caution to the wind. Just as he opened his mouth to explain the door bell rang.

"I bet that's your aunt. Why don't you go down and let her in?"

Daniel looked at his father sideways before running down the stairs.

"Stop running, please." Allen called out to Daniel. He was relieved to be able to skate by that incident, yet he knew the conversation would rise again. Daniel was a lot like him, wouldn't stop until he got an answer that satisfied his curiosity.

"Hey, there handsome," Yolanda sang. Two years younger, at thirty-five, Yolanda didn't look a day over twenty-one. A petite woman, Yolanda's hour-glass figure and smooth cocoa face had always been something that men drooled over. Many a day, Allen and Tim fought just about every boy in their old neighborhood over inappropriate comments, glares or touches. And the two of them had always been close, more so after Donna left, followed by the tragic death of Yolanda's husband in a car accident two years earlier.

"Hey, good lookin'. What cha got cookin'?" he sang as he kissed his sister on the cheek.

"Must be some date?"

Daniel snickered. "I'll say, Auntie! He's been in that mirror for an hour. And, he's changed shirts . . . ." Daniel began counting on his narrow brown fingers. He held up three fingers and then four.

"That many, ugh? Must be special." Yolanda eyed Allen as he slipped his feet into a pair of deep olive green captoe shoes, adjusted the collar on his cream colored mock turtle neck sweater, followed by buckling the olive green belt over his worsted wool olive slacks.

"Daniel, why don't you go down to the kitchen and get your favorite aunt something to drink."

"Oh, boy, it's time for grown folk's talk. I get the hint."

Allen watched as Yolanda chased Daniel out of the room with a swat on his backside. They waited until his footsteps could no longer be heard. Allen faced the mirror, his sister's reflection stared at him as she sat on the bed.

"Okay, Casanova, what gives?" she asked.

"Nothing." He tried to hide his smile. "Why does something have to be up?"

"Well, for one, Daniel told me you had a 'special date' tonight. And two, you don't normally change clothes so many times." Yolanda picked up two shirts, a sweater and a pair of slacks from the floor and slung them behind her onto the bed.

"I wasn't sure what I wanted to wear. That's all."

"Come on, Allen. You know you can't keep secrets from me. You know I'll find out sooner or later."

"Yo, there's nothing to tell."

But he knew what she said was true. He could never keep secrets from her, and he figured there was no sense in trying now. He wondered if he should tell her the whole story, including his date with Kayla. Allen watched his sister as she began nosing about his room. She picked up cologne bottles, sniffed, then picked up a collar bar, looked it over before placing it back on top of the chest of drawers. He twirled around when he spied her picking up Kayla's charm bracelet.

"Wow. This is nice. Who did you buy it for?"

He walked over and took the bracelet out of Yolanda's hand. "I didn't buy it. It belongs to Kayla."

Yolanda let out a gasp. "The Kayla?" her eyes widened.

"Yup."

Yolanda jumped on the bed and landed squarely in its middle.

"What?" he asked.

"Aw, come on Allen. When did you see her?"

"About a week ago," he began as he walked over to the dresser and picked up a bottle of cologne. He turned and motioned the bottle toward Yolanda.

"Yeah, wear that one. The scent is really sexy," Yolanda responded offhandedly. "So, tell me all about it. I mean don't leave a word out!"

"Jeez, Yolanda," he said. "I feel like we're in high school again."

"So what?! I want to know. You know I'm nosy."

He knew he wouldn't be able to get out of the house without at least feeding some of his sister's curiosity.

"I saw Kayla last week. She got splashed by some cab driver and I took her home."

"She got splashed and I took her home." Yolanda mocked him in a taunting singsong voice. "And that's all?"

"She dropped this in the car." He held the bracelet up. "And she's meeting me tonight for dinner so I can return it to her." He walked back to the full length mirror, nodded and turned to face Yolanda, his arms outstretched. He waited for her approval.

"You look good." Yolanda nodded. "But, wait. Just so I'm clear. This is the one and only Kayla you dated many moons ago?"

"Yup. The one and only."

"Dang. She must be desperate." Yolanda laughed, then scrambled off the bed and ran toward the stairs. Allen ran behind her.

Daniel stood at the foot of the stairs. "No running."

Yolanda and Allen laughed.

"True that, little man, true that," he said and lifted Daniel up into his arms. "Now, you be good and listen to your aunt. I want a favorable report when I return."

"Are you going to bring me back a doggy bag?" Daniel asked while he stroked the side of Allen's clean shaven face.

"They're called 'leftovers,' and yes, if there is something left over I'll bring it to you. But when I return, you should be in bed and sound asleep."

"Come on, Daddy. It's Friday. There's no school tomorrow. Can't I stay up until you get back?" Daniel whined.

He placed Daniel on the floor and squatted to be face to face with his son. "No can do. You have to be in bed no later than midnight. How's that?"

Daniel nodded and stood next to Yolanda.

"Have a good time, Dad. We want to hear all about it."

Allen kissed Daniel on the cheek, patted Yolanda on the arm and headed to his car.

Chapter 9

"Well, I do believe that will get his attention," Amina giggled and stuffed popcorn into her mouth.

Kayla shook her head and wondered why she even asked Amina to come over to help her find something to wear for her "outing" with Allen.

"And I don't know why you keep calling it an 'outing', it's a date. Plain and simple, its a date," Amina stated.

"Amina, ain't it about time you went home?"

"Can't. My brother is painting my place. Can't stand those fumes. They make me sick." Amina swallowed a large gulp of soda. "Besides, I wouldn't miss this for the world. Kayla got a date. A real live date."

"Behave," she admonished, then changed the subject. "What time is it? Allen is supposed to be here by seven." Kayla looked over at the clock. She was nervous, fidgety.

"Girl, you got half an hour." Amina sniffed. "You better finish up, though. I'll get your coat."

"Get the fur jacket."

"You gonna wear a hat?" Amina asked as she danced out of the bedroom and headed to the spare bedroom.

"Naw, I have a black shawl I'll wear over my head. It's hanging near the jacket," Kayla called after Amina. She heard Amina open the closet door, followed by the sound of the stereo.

"What you wanna hear?"

"Who said I wanted to listen to some music?" Kayla called back.

"It'll put you in the mood. How about some Whispers?"

Kayla refused to respond. Why respond when she knew that Amina wanted to hear those crooning brothers, Walt and Scotty, sing "It's A Love Thing." And sure enough, the smooth synthesizer, followed by a heavy drum beat announced the song. As hard as she tried, Kayla couldn't help smiling and bobbing her head to the intro of the song.

"It's a love thang," Kayla began singing along. "It's a love thang."

"It's a la-ah-aah-love thang. Thang!" Amina added, her deep sultry voice mimicking the group as she returned to Kayla's bedroom with the fur jacket and shawl. Amina placed them on the bed and they both stepped into a slide, shaking their hips to the beat. Kayla picked up her hair brush and started singing the chorus — its words telling of how one's heart beats with love.

"Go on girl! Sing that song," Amina yelled as she began shimmying around the bedroom, her hands raised above her head. She slowed and put on Kayla's fur jacket, then picked up where she left off without missing a beat. The two danced like that for nearly the whole length of the song as they sang the refrain and chorus.

"Girl." Amina stopped, her right hand on her hip, her left hand gesturing as if she was in church listening to some testimony, "them boys can sing. You know that's what Allen is gonna be saying after he gets a look at you in that outfit. That bad fella is sharp. Turn around."

Kayla twirled around, her head still moved to the beat of the song. She faced the mirror. The winter white two-piece angora outfit was perfect, the ankle length skirt had a split that rode daringly up the right side of her leg, exposing an ample amount of her thigh.

"Girl, I like this coat, too," Amina commented. Her hands ran up and down the front of the black and gray racoon jacket. Kayla looked at her, thinking that it complemented her warm sepia complexion perfectly.

"You look good, girl. You should get you one. Adrianna Furs got a sale going on. I'm thinking about trading in my mink for another one."

"Yeah, I might just do that." Amina pulled the full collar up around her neck. "You ever fear that some idiot will put paint on your coat?"

Kayla put her hands on her hips and faced Amina. "Hell, girl, I wish one of those zealots would!"

Amina gave her a high five. Kayla looked at the clock.

"Damn, Amina, he'll be here any minute!" She ran to her closet, pulled out her bone colored high-heeled boots and nearly fell over as she attempted to put the boots on standing up.

"Slow down, girl. You gonna break something." Amina laughed. "Besides, let him wait a few minutes. Nothing wrong with that."

"You know I hate to be late."

"Will you listen to me this one time?" Amina asked. "It will give him something to think about — imagine what you're wearing. You know, some anticipation?"

Kayla looked at her friend, sat on the bed, and slowly put her boots on. She walked to the mirror, turned left then right.

"Gosh, this outfit makes my behind look humongous."

"Only a dog likes a bone," Amina stated as she took another sip of her soda.

"Is there any soda left?"

"Umm, I think I saved you a corner," Amina replied. "I'll get it for you. How much you want?"

"Just half a glass."

She stared at her reflection. She liked what she saw. Her complexion glowed and her dark eyes were complemented by the light brown highlights of her shoulder length hair. Despite her own earlier arguments with herself, Kayla had her hair and nails done expressly for her date with Allen. It had been a long time and a lot of bad blood between them, but she was ready to face him, let him see what he had so foolishly given up. She nodded at the fitted two-piece. Its matching v-neck tunic gave enough of a peek at her cleavage to be daring. When she heard the sound of the doorbell, she broke out into a cold sweat. The tunic began to stick to her back.

"It's only an outing," she reminded herself. "To get my bracelet back."

"You want me to answer that?" Amina called out.

She didn't respond. She knew Amina was already at the door. Then she heard Amina's voice, all sugary and sweet, speak into the intercom. "Come on up."

Kayla finished with a gold watch on her wrist and her three favorite rings on her fingers. One ruby, her birth stone, set in a simple gold band, a diamond cluster on her right index finger and another ruby, a small solitaire surrounded by diamond baguets on her left ring finger. She looked at that one. It stood as a symbol that said she would never marry again.

She stole one last glance at her reflection, grabbed her coat, purse and shawl, and headed toward the living room, where Allen was waiting.

"This is going to be some outing," Kayla told herself.

Allen was chatting when Kayla appeared in the living room. He smiled, absorbing the way the cream-colored outfit brought out the warm smoothness of her skin tone. He paused momentarily at the sounds of a synthesizer seeped from the overhead speakers and introduced Isaac Hayes' "Look of Love." He remembered it was one of Kayla's favorite songs.

"You're looking good, Kayla," Allen said as he stood and walked over to stand in front of her. He bent slightly, kissed her on the cheek, then handed her a bouquet of mixed flowers.

"You too," she returned the compliment, then took the flowers from him. "But, then again you always did look good in your clothes."

"Why thank you," Allen blushed. "You ready?"

Kayla nodded, handing Amina the flowers. Allen held her fur and as she slipped into it, he allowed his hands to rest momentarily on her shoulders before she looked back at him, her head tilted slightly to one side. He tried to read her — tried to gauge her expression. He needed some hint, some clue as to how the evening would progress. She gave none, her emotions firmly held inside of her. Allen guided her to the door.

"Have a good time." Amina called to them, waving as they left the loft and walked down the corridor toward the elevator.

"That's a nice fur you've got there. A steal?"

Kayla smiled. "No, I didn't steal it. It was a bargain though. I watched this coat for months. Waited for it to go on sale."

"You were always good at waiting for bargains."

Kayla looked directly at Allen. "Yeah, but some bargains aren't worth waiting for."

He dismissed her obvious meaning. "I hope you like Cajun. I know this great little place downtown. Serves some of the best Gumbo this side of Cajun Country itself."

"I do. But it's the really hot stuff I can't get with."

He held the car door and watched her swing her shapely legs inside. He stole a glimpse of a toned thigh. Sucking in his breath, he closed the door and ordered himself to behave.

To Allen, the short fifteen minute ride to the restaurant seemed to take forever. Kayla had only nodded her head in response to his litany of questions. At the restaurant, he watched as she picked at her food, looking at him only once when he called her by name. He didn't like the way the evening was going. He wanted her to at least be more cordial, more amenable to their date. Sure, ten years is a long time and in that time he knew a lot had gone on in both of their lives. And yes, he knew she was angry, but he felt that if she would just get it out, curse him, yell at him, then at least he would know how she felt — where he stood with her.

"Oh, here's your bracelet." Allen handed it over to her as they waited for the valet to bring his car.

"Thanks. And thanks for dinner," she responded indifferently.

Allen was quiet. He decided to reserve his comment for when they got into the car.

When the valet pulled up and parked, Allen tipped him and moved around to the passenger side and held open the door. He had to admit that he wanted one more look at Kayla's shapely legs.

He got behind the wheel and peeled from the curb. He gunned the engine as he skillfully motioned around slower moving vehicles. Then quickly turning off onto a side street, he skidded to a stop and placed the car in park.

Kayla blinked at him.

"All night you've been silent. Nodding like some dime store figurine. Answering my questions with simple one word replies. If you didn't want to go out with me, why didn't you say so?"

Kayla turned her body completely around in her seat to face Allen. He could see the fire in her eyes.

"Now ain't' this something!" Kayla began through clinched teeth. "So, you came rushing in on your white horse when I was in distress, and I appreciated the rescue. But really, Allen, after ten years, do you seriously believe that we are going to just pick up where we left off?! I mean, damn, Allen, you left me. No explanation, other than some tired-assed garbage about you needing space and you weren't the man for me. You have no idea how it affected me. I cried for what seemed like an eternity, and now you want me to be all good with this? Man, you are either on dope or dog food! And its got to be dope, 'cause dog food don't make you crazy!"

Kayla turned her body and sat straight, her face forward, her eyes blinked rapidly. Without warning, tears began to stream down her face, and before long she sat sobbing quietly.

"You really hurt me, Allen," she whispered. "How can I ever forget that?"

He touched her face and gently pulled her closer to him. He kissed her cheek, the heat from the tears burned into his soul. He brushed her hair from her face and softly kissed her again.

"Let me make it up to you, Kayla," he breathed, then wrapped his arms around her and pulled her as close as the middle console would allow.

"How can I say I'm sorry? What can I do?" he whispered and held her tighter. He never wanted to let her go. "I know I hurt you. Tell me, sweetheart, what can I do to make it up to you?"

Kayla blinked back more tears. "Please Allen, take me home."

Chapter 10

Allen drove slowly as he tried to gather his thoughts. His feelings. He knew what had happened between them had hurt her, he just didn't fully realize how much it still affected her until he saw her tears. Now all he wanted was a chance to make it up to her. To have her in his life again. But how? Allen wondered as he pulled up in front of Kayla's building.

She opened the passenger's door and without a word got out and headed toward her building. He followed her and stood next to her at the elevator.

"I've got to make sure you make it in all right. Do you mind?" he said in response to her harsh glare. He knew it was just his own feeble excuse to buy him more time with her, make this whole situation right.

Kayla shook her head as the elevator stopped on her floor. She retrieved her keys from her purse, opened the door and stepped inside. Allen moved past her and began to inspect her apartment, her cat followed close behind. He spotted the fireplace, a low fire burning. He figured Amina had lit the fire.

"Where's your girl?"

"I guess she left. Why?"

"No reason, just wondering."

"Well does everything check out, Officer Dawson?" Kayla asked snidely. Allen nodded in response. "Good, then you can go back to whatever rock you crawled out from under."

"Ouch," Allen said, looking squarely at her. He wanted her to be with him. He wanted to show her he had changed. That he could be and was the man she wanted.

"Allen, I don't think you heard me? You can leave now."

"I'm not leaving until we settle this. I know I was wrong. But until you hear me out, I'm not leaving. You have to hear my side of this. You have to understand how I was feeling back then. The fear. The uncertainty."

Kayla shrugged her shoulders and sat down on the chaise in her living room. When Allen moved to sit next to her, she quickly put her feet up.

"Fine. I'll sit over here," Allen said as he sat on the sofa near by.

"Kayla, ten years is a long time, I know this. But in that time a lot has happened to me. A lot of pain and a lot of growing. I have a son," Allen watched Kayla's expression turn from disinterest to curiosity. He knew he could continue. "Daniel is eight, almost nine. I got married almost a year after we broke up."

"We?"

"Okay, after I broke up with you."

"Where's his mother?" Kayla asked. Allen could hear a hint of jealousy in her voice.

"That's a good question," he responded, then raked his hand over his closely cut hair. "She disappeared about six months after Daniel was born. It's been just the two of us ever since. But in that time, I've come to see what's important and what's not. And sometimes the fear you feel isn't nearly as important as letting those close to you know how you feel. Daniel taught me that." Allen paused. He noticed that Kayla's face had softened, the pain he witnessed earlier had begun to ebb. He continued. "Kayla, I was afraid back then. Afraid of love. Afraid of commitment. Afraid of how you made me feel. I didn't want to believe that anything as good as we had existed. So, I ran. I ran, pretending, telling myself . . . no, I tried to make myself believe that I didn't love you. And all the while I did, and I believe I still do." He tilted his head to the right. Allen noticed that her expression had changed. He decided to finish. "I know I can't take back what happened, can't turn back the hands of time. Lord knows I wish I could. But I can only go forward and hope that you will accept my apology. Kayla, will you forgive me? Can you forgive me?"

"Allen?" Kayla stood. He watched her closely, her hands clasped tightly together. "How many times over the years have I wanted an explanation. Anything that would have allowed me to just move on — to put some closure to us so that I could be whole. You robbed me of that." She walked away and stood in the window, her back to him. "Allen, I had to fight my own feelings just to try and go on with my life. It wasn't fair, Allen, it just wasn't fair." She thought of how much she had loved him, let her mind retrace the steps to the first time they made love, thoughts of the precious gift she had given him — herself. She shut her eyes and let that warm Indian summer day ten years ago replay for what seemed like the millionth time.

The evening had started like most of the Friday nights they spent together — a trip to Goose Island for a large bag of jumbo shrimp, fried mushrooms and zucchini, then on to one of their many secluded spots. This night it was on the roof top of his apartment building. To Kayla, there was something in the air that surrounded them — said things were going to be different between the two of them. She instinctively knew that their relation was going to change forever.

When Allen had picked her up at the house she shared with her father and sister, there was a strange look on his face. Nothing sinister, or threatening, just something she couldn't decipher. When they arrived at his apartment, then made their way to the top, Kayla became nervous. Not a frightening nervousness, but a giddy one. Allen carried a blanket under his arm and a portable radio/tape player in one hand and held her hand in the other.

He spread the blanket out on the black tarp, turned on the tape player and took Kayla's hand in his. As the slow music filled the space around them, he led Kayla into a slow dance, singing the words to LTD's "Love Ballad" lowly into her ear. She laid her head on his chest, closed her eyes and listened to the rhythmic sound of his heart.

"Kayla, do you know that I'm absolutely crazy about you?" he whispered into her ear. "I have been since the first time I met you. I didn't know it then, but I know it now. I love you. You hear me, Miss Kayla Martin? I'm in love with you."

She nodded, afraid that if she spoke her words would break the spell of his admission of love and the effects they were having on her. For the last six months, she had wanted to hear him say those words, to confirm that his feelings matched hers. When she felt his body tense, she stepped back and watched the distant lights from Chicago's city scape dance in his eyes as a mixture of fear and uncertainty settled there. She had to tell him. Had to let him know she felt as he did and never wanted this night, this feeling to end.

He spoke again. "But, I understand if it's too soon. You don't have to tell me how you feel just because I said what I did."

"No, Allen. I do."

Allen looked at Kayla hard. "You do what?"

"I love you, Allen," she admitted and took his face in her hands. He kissed her, slightly at first, his lips lingering upon hers. Then with more urgency, he pressed past her lips to find her tongue. She moaned loudly. A sensation inside of her awakened — one she had never felt before — and she wrapped her arms about his neck, pulling him closer to her. She could feel the hardened length of him strain against the cloth that separated them, that kept them from being one.

Allen broke the kiss.

"Kayla, I want to make love to you."

She didn't know how to respond. She wanted him, but how could she tell him. She hadn't the words to impress upon him how badly she too wanted to make love with him.

"Kayla? Did you hear me?"

She cleared her throat. "Yes Allen. I want you."

He sat down on the blanket and extended his hand to her. She accepted it and sat down beside him. Stroking her face, he let his hands absorb the smoothness of her skin. Kayla began to shiver as he traced long paths down her face, across her back and around to her high, firm breasts. He gently pushed the strings of her tank-top down across her shoulders, revealing her bare skin. Slight goose bumps rose, as Allen began seductively kissing her shoulders before letting his tongue trace circles across the tops of her full, high breasts. Kayla threw her head back as Allen's deliberate motions became more intense.

Lowering her onto the blanket, Allen continued kissing her, this time letting his soft hands trail up and down her thighs, resting occasionally on her flat abdomen. Kayla opened her eyes to see the full moon over his shoulders. The stars were like sprinkles of dust across the deep blue sky.

"Kayla, you are so beautiful. All I think about is you. Tell me. Is this real or are you playing with me?"

"Allen, this is real. I love you." She pulled him on top of her, feeling his full weight rest upon her body and began to move to the rise and fall of his breath in her ear.

"Are you sure?" Allen paused.

"I'm sure."

He rose and began removing his clothes, until he was fully naked. Kayla had never seen a naked man up close. She let her eyes steal furtive glances at his perfectly chiseled body. His large arms tapered into a wide chest attached to a well-formed six-pack abdomen. She wanted to examine him up close, to feel the thickness of him.

Allen watched her. Tried to gauge the expression on her face. This was always difficult — always hard for him. He had slept with a few women, so that wasn't the problem. Exposing his emotions was the problem. But now, things were too far gone to go back, to stop the love, the passion that had built over the months.

He began to methodically undress her, first pulling her tank-top over her head, followed by her skirt and underwear. He took in the full view of Kayla's nakedness in the light of the moon, then began to kiss and nibble on her neck and breasts.

"Allen, please," Kayla breathed, reaching out for him, wanting him to stop the mellifluous torture coming from his lips and tongue.

"Please what, my dear?" Allen whispered, teasing Kayla with his tongue as he made a trail down her breasts, across her abdomen to her spot. When he let his lips circle then enclose her pearl, Kayla groaned loudly, moving her hips to the heightened feeling.

It swept her up, causing a sweet shudder across her entire body. She tensed and held onto Allen's shoulders as she let out a long continuous sigh, signaling to him that she was ready for the next sweep.

Allen removed a foil package from a nearby bag, moved over Kayla's body and prepared to enter her. He stopped suddenly at the resistence.

"Is this your, umm?"

"Yes, Allen. You are the first."

"I don't want to hurt you."

"You won't. Just love me, Allen. Love me." Her hands roamed across his chest — pausing to tease the nipples surrounded by wisps of hair. He kissed Kayla full on the lips, adjusted his weight to wrap his arms around her and held onto her tightly, his face nestled along hers. Reluctantly, he released her only long enough to enter her slowly, calculating his movement. He desperately wanted this moment, this night to be as special for her as it was for him. He pressed forward, then paused to look into her eyes. When she moved her hips into his, he continued. Kayla let out a small gasp, pulling her hips back.

"Are you okay?" Allen whispered. "I don't want to hurt you."

Kayla mumbled, nodding her head. She stilled for a moment, letting the foreign sensation creep into her being. A wondrous feeling slid over her entire body as she began to move her hips in circular motions, then back and forward. She quivered as she wrapped her arms and then her legs around Allen. She wanted him closer, to intertwine with her body and soul.

They began to move in unison, their breathing coming in long labored moans, as their bodies thrust into each other. They held each other tightly. Kayla began to groan deeply as the sensation took over. Her body had reacted in ways she had never thought possible. And the more she groaned the more Allen moved until suddenly she reached her second orgasm all while calling out his name and professing her love for him into the warm Indian summer night. Allen groaned loudly as his own passion erupted.

And she had cried. Not tears of pain, but of simple joy from being loved by Allen — an unmistakable love that she didn't think would ever fade, but that would only get stronger as time passed. How wrong she had been.

Kayla was brought back to the present with Allen's slow movement toward her. He stood behind her. His scent swirled around them, his voice came out shaky.

"I know I hurt you Kayla and ever since I've regretted, experienced pure anguish over my decision. Not a day goes by, hasn't gone by, when my heart isn't heavy with how I treated you. How I broke our relationship into pieces, but Kayla you still haven't answered my questions. How can I make it up to you? And will you accept my apology?" He turned her to face him.

"I don't know, Allen. I've changed a lot."

"That I can see."

"What can you see?"

"You're more self-assured," he responded.

"Oh? One date and you can tell?"

"Aw, come on now, Kayla. Don't play me like that."

She winced. "True. You were always very intuitive. You could pick up on people with a snap."

Allen looked out the window, over Kayla's head. His feet felt as if they were glued to the floor, her scent wreaked havoc with his senses. He still knew her, the very essence of her, and that cologne — Chaos — her signature fragrance, swept across his being like the warmth of a summer breeze. *How did I ever let her go?* He wondered as he lowered his gaze upon her profile.

Kayla moved from the window and returned to the chaise. Allen smiled slightly when he noticed that this time she had kept her feet on the floor.

"I want to hear more about your son. Does he look like you?"

Allen joined her and pulled pictures of Daniel out of his wallet.

"My God, he looks just like you. Like you spit him out."

"Yeah, his mother used to say that." Allen's voice trailed off. Kayla touched his arm.

"Allen, why did his mother leave?"

He rubbed the growing stubble on his face. He wanted to be honest with her.

"She said that I didn't love her, that I loved you. And that she couldn't fight my ghosts any more."

He waited for Kayla to respond, to say something. Instead, he felt her small hand massage the length of his arm. He faced her — her eyes stared into his.

"I'm sorry to hear that, Allen. It must be tough raising a child alone."

"Well, my mom and Yolanda help out quite a bit. Yolanda's at the house now. She's his favorite."

"How are your mom and your sisters?"

"Well, mom is fine. My dad died about five years ago. At first we were concerned about her, but after about a year, she started getting out, started traveling. And you know how Tim's been faring."

She looked squarely at him, intent on making him the one to end the silly game. "I do?"

"Yes, you do, Kayla. We can stop pretending now. I know he's been your mechanic for years."

"Oh, well yes. I kind of figured you knew." Kayla's voice caught in her throat. Finally. She chuckled. "And here I was thinking I was swearing that man to secrecy. So much for that."

"Don't be mad at him. I completely understand."

Kayla changed the subject. "How's Yolanda?"

"Unfortunately, her husband was killed in an auto accident a couple of years back. God rest his soul. They were planning on kids, but never had any, so Daniel is like her own. She spoils him something rotten. And with the exception of Yolanda, everybody else lives out-of-state and is doing well with three kids each."

"Wow, that's a lot of nieces and nephews," Kayla responded.

"Yeah, Christmas is a riot. They all come home then. And it makes mom happy to have us all under one roof. This year we're going to do grab bags, because there are just too many of us for one person to buy everybody an individual gift."

"Well, we don't have that problem. Ours is just the opposite. If Dad, Laura and I each bought one gift, the tree would be bare," Kayla laughed, removed her boots, tossing them carelessly into a corner, stood, then started toward what Allen assumed was the kitchen. "Would you like something to drink?" She called out.

"What do you have?" Allen responded, absently. He was finally glad to know that the other initial on her bracelet didn't belong to Jonathan. That was one obstacle he didn't want to face, but knew he would if forced to.

"Come and see," Kayla called back.

Allen watched her bend over, her head ducked into the refrigerator. He forced himself to focus his attention on her voice as she called off a variety of items to drink.

"I'll take the Corona. You got some lime?"

"Sure do." She handed him the bottle. "Can't have Corona's and no lime."

"This is a nice place."

"You want the ten-cent tour?"

He nodded his head and followed her as she took him around her loft. When he brushed up against her, she didn't move. He took her in his arms and kissed her gently.

"Umm, Allen," she broke the embrace. "I think its a little soon for all of this. Don't you?"

"Yeah, you're right. Where are my manners?" He held up his hands, then stepped back. She continued the tour, ending at her bedroom. He was impressed with the large mahogany sleigh bed. The room was decorated in muted tones of cream, teal and gold. He liked her taste, it wasn't overly feminine — he could see himself becoming quite comfortable in her place.

"Oh, well that's it," Kayla said, returning to the living room.

For the rest of the evening they talked about the past, where they had been, and where they wanted to go. They even laughed at past dating situations. Still Allen wondered when she would bring up Jonathan. He resolved to let her mention her ex-husband. One step at a time, he told himself, one step at a time.

Finally, Allen looked at the LED clock on the VCR. "Kayla, its getting late. I better be going now."

"Oh my!" Kayla looked at the clock. "Yes, it is late. Well, thank you for dinner."

"No, thank you for this opportunity," he replied as he stood. She helped him with his coat and opened the door.

"Good night, Allen. Drive safely."

"I will," he kissed her on the cheek and stepped out into the foyer. He heard the door shut behind him. He turned and knocked. Kayla opened the door and looked into Allen's eyes.

"Kayla, will you go out with me again?"

"I guess it would be all right, Allen, but let's take it slow for now. Okay?"

"Sure. I'll talk to you soon. Goodnight."

The jangling sound of the phone startled Kayla. She looked at the caller ID and saw Allen's name appear. She smiled.

"Hello?"

"It's just me. I made it home."

"Good. I'm glad you thought to call. You know, to let me know you made it in one piece."

"Kayla, thanks for letting me clear the air. It's what I've needed to do for years."

"So have I, Allen. So have I."

"I won't keep you, sweetheart. Nite, Kayla, sweet dreams."

She hung up. She couldn't believe that she had gone out with Allen Dawson — and she let him kiss her. His lips were still soft. The passion in his embrace and the sincerity in his words shone in his eyes. She felt that all she had ever wanted was an explanation, a reason why.

Kayla thought of all the unanswered questions she once had. The feelings of things left unsaid — unresolved. Now she had her answers. He seemed to have become everything she wanted in a man: strong, sensuous, unafraid and honest. She wondered if it were his son that might have changed him, or was it just maturity? Yes, she felt he had truly changed.

She made up her mind. She would take it one day at a time, because, in truth, she knew in her heart that she and Allen were far from over. Still, the pain and fear of their breakup wouldn't stop gnawing at her. What if he ran again? Kayla wasn't sure she could handle rejection from him a second time.

A vicious chill ran up her body. The last thing she wanted was to feel that type of pain again.

She turned off her light and climbed into bed. Images of Allen's kiss and strong arms about her danced in her head. She rolled over on her side, forced the images from her mind and willed herself to sleep.

Allen set the phone in its cradle and peered through the vertical blinds out across the street. He thought he had seen someone move into the shadows and it gave him an odd feeling. He tried to dismiss the whole thing, but there was a nagging voice that told him to keep his guard up.

He crept up the stairs and paused at Daniel's room. He pushed open the partially closed door and peeked around it. He smiled as he watched Daniel sleep, the covers kicked around the base of his feet. He tipped further into the room, stopped at his bed and pulled the covers up around his son's shoulders. He kissed him on the cheek and turned to leave.

"Hey, Daddy, did you have fun?" Daniel asked in a sleepy voice.

"Yes, I did," Allen whispered. "Now go back to sleep."

"Nite, Daddy."

"Nite, little man. I love you."

"Me too."

He watched from the doorway as Daniel turned on his side. He waited until he heard his familiar breathing, the one that signaled he was asleep, then he walked softly to his home office. Yolanda was asleep on the day bed, a soft snore escaped her partially open lips. He resisted the temptation to put his hand over her mouth, like he did when they were kids. Instead, he covered her with a blanket, turned off the small lamp nearby and left the room.

He walked to his room and shut his door. He undressed down to his black jockey briefs and sat on the edge of the bed. His senses reeled as they recalled the sweet fragrance of Kayla's perfume, her tender lips when he kissed her.

Finally the night had gotten better, especially when she allowed him to come inside her loft. He knew immediately that this was his opportunity, his chance to tell her why he left and how he felt about her. At first she was stunned, he saw it on her face, and he knew that he had made some strides. But he could also see that she was still hurt and that made him angry. Not angry at her, but angry that he had wasted so much time when they could have been together all along.

He pulled back the covers and slipped between the sheets. He rested his arms behind his head. Yeah, tonight was just the beginning.   He was sure of it.   Oh, yes, Ms. Kayla, tonight was only the beginning.

Chapter 11

Kayla stretched her long arms up and outward as she climbed out of bed. A satisfied grin spread across her face when she thought of Allen. He told her he had a surprise for her, and she loved surprises. She looked at the clock.

"It's almost 8:30," she said. "He said he would be here at 10:00."

She looked around her room at her unmade bed and the clothes that lay carelessly on the floor and across her chaise longue. One hour was what she knew she had to jump in the shower and be dressed by the time Allen arrived. She began to straighten up her room. She let her imagination wander in and out of every possible scenario, with each one ending with her locked in Allen's arms.

For over a month, she had seen Allen just about every other day, and she had been astonished by his wit, charm and his unending attention. She didn't feel smothered, like she had with the countless other dates she had been on. They all paled in comparison to Allen, for no one had shown her the kind of affection that he was showering upon her, and she had to admit that she was loving every minute of it.

"Music." Kayla picked up her cat, Patton, and carried her to the den. "I need some music." She turned on the stereo, put in the new CD Allen had bought her, and began to sway. He knew how much she liked music, all types, from Yanni, to Dance Hall Reggae, to Old School compilations, Kayla loved music. But it was this CD that she had come to play just about every morning. Jeffery Osborne's ultimate collection held songs that seemed to elicit good memories. Yet, there was one in particular — one Allen had played when he first gave her the CD.

"Here," he had said. "Let's listen to this one first."

She had watched him as he placed the CD in the player, then tapped the selection button until smooth strings and percussions filtered out of the overhead speakers in her loft. Allen walked slowly toward her and put his hand out. He pulled her to him and locked his arms about her waist. Kayla laid her head on his chest as they began to sway slowly from side to side, their bodies close while he sang softly in her ear. His deep baritone matched Jeffery's as the words to the song announced "Love Ballad." It had been their song, the one they had made love to the very first time.

Kayla breathed deeply, the memory of his touch, his scent surrounded her as her mind traveled back to the time when she had loved him so very much. Back then, she had shown him the depth of her emotions the only way she knew how, by sharing herself with him. She shuddered slightly, the reflections of their love making sweet and warm. The next time they made love, they had done so at the beach. He had laid her gently on a blanket, and slowly removed her clothes. The waves from Lake Michigan were in sync with

their love making. A high, full moon shone on their bodies.
She knew he loved her then, completely and fully. And she
realized there had been no love like it since. Could they love
like that again?

"Kayla, I remembered this song," he had whispered in
her ear, pulling her out of the seduction of her memory. "And
it's true, what we have is much more than they can see."

They continued to dance, their movements slower.
Allen had kissed her, lightly at first, then with an urgency, a
fever she had never known from him, even the first time.

To her, it was all so surreal, like she was in a dream, yet
when she began to kiss him back, her hands caressing the
sides of his smooth face, she knew this was all too real. She
released herself from his embrace and stared up into his eyes.
The look was unmistakable, the intensity they held let her
know, once again, that their relationship was about to take a
turn, was about to forever change. She inched away.

"Kayla, I'm not going anywhere." He seemed to read her
mind. "I . . ." He had stammered. "I want you. Here. Now.
Forever." He took her hand. "Do you know that?"

She nodded.

"But only when you are ready. I won't push," he had
replied, letting her hand drop to her side, then gathered his
things and left.

She was in the midst of a dream, her dream, as she
danced with Patton secured in her arms. Then stopping suddenly, she placed her cat on the floor. She pushed the pause
button on the remote, stopping the song in mid stream. The

revelation hit her, hard, and though she had tried to keep her emotions in check, she could no longer deny that she was madly in love with Allen.

Kayla slowly lowered her body to sit on the futon. So much had happened to her, from her loveless marriage to Jonathan, to the endless dates with men she cared little or nothing about. Over the years, she knew she had been going though the motions, just existing and not living her life with passion. She glanced at the wall where she had hung a large poster with the mantra, "The Essence of Passion," written boldly at the bottom. She read the verse over and again, and knew it was time. Time to live her life as if it would end tomorrow. Not with reckless abandon, but without fear and reservation. Yeah, she thought, that was easier said than done, for she was a rambling testament to that fact.

Her mind wandered to Allen. Loving him, being in love with him, frightened her. She didn't want him to run, but she didn't want him to stop pursuing her either. Her thoughts of him were now more pleasant, invoking a warm, mushy feeling each time his handsome face appeared. She wondered if he felt the same intensity, and if he didn't, could she handle it. The sound of the phone ringing interrupted her thoughts. She sighed and picked it up.

"Hello."

"Hey beautiful," Jonathan spoke into the receiver. "How are you this morning?"

Kayla bit her bottom lip. "I'm okay. And you?"

"Well, I'm better now that I'm hearing your voice."

"Jonathan, you really should stop calling me."

"Why? You got some other brother over there?" She heard him snicker, as if he knew that there was no one with her, but what he didn't know was that she had given her heart, again, to the man she truly loved. She shook her head, then rolled her eyes upward. Yes, it was time, and though she didn't want to be rude to him, Kayla knew she had to make Jonathan move on — get on with his life without her.

"Jonathan," Kayla began. "We've been divorced for a long time. Don't you have someone special in your life?

"Kayla, there will never be another like you. What can I do to convince you of this?" he responded as she sighed out loud. "What is it Kayla? Have you found someone else? Is that it?" Suddenly, his voice became harsh, chilling.

"Well." Kayla stopped. She hated explaining herself, but she also knew that her cowardly treatment of Jonathan hadn't been right. She needed to finally settle things between them, get him to let her go. "I have, Jonathan. I'm in love."

Kayla pulled the phone from her ear. "Never!" She heard Jonathan bark into the phone. "Who is it?"

"Jonathan, stop this!"

"Never, Kayla." His voice became light, almost sinister. "I'll never let you go. Do you hear me? Besides, you owe me, Kayla. I know you were in love with that loser, Allen, when we married. But he wasn't even man enough to tell you the truth. Tell me its not him. Tell me its someone else? Anyone but him!"

Kayla shut her eyes. There was just no way this was Jonathan. He was always so mild mannered and laid back. When they were married, she could never get a reaction from him. He had always shrugged his shoulders and ignored any emotions he wasn't interested in. Now, here he was screaming like a mad man one minute, then all calm the next. Her guard went up — this wasn't at all like the Jonathan she knew.

"Jonathan," Kayla began smoothly. "You have to move on. I've moved on. I'm seeing someone else and its pretty serious."

"Kayla, you didn't answer my question. Is it Allen?"

"That's none of your business," she snapped.

"You just answered my question," he responded. "How could you give him another chance? After the way he hurt you? You know, and I know, that Allen Dawson doesn't give a shit about you. He's just trying to see if he can get you back, then he'll drop you so fast your head will spin."

"Jonathan, you don't know what you're talking about."

"Yeah, right. If you say so. But Kayla, you and Allen won't be together for long. Not if I can help it, you won't be. I'll personally see to it, Kayla. Mark my words." He hung up.

This was all some sick dream. How in the hell had Jonathan turned so belligerent? Kayla put her face in her hands. This was all her fault and she knew it. Had she just insisted he not call her, he wouldn't be acting like this.

She rose and headed toward the bathroom. The phone rang again. She picked it up slowly.

"Hello?"

"Hey, Sister. What's up this beautiful morning?" Amina sang.

Kayla let her breath out. She was relieved it was Amina and not Jonathan again.

"Not a whole lot. About to get into the shower. Allen's going to be here at 10:00. What are you up to?"

"Well, well, now, aren't we getting cozy? Where are you two heading to today?"

"I don't know. Allen wouldn't tell me. He said it was a surprise."

Amina laughed. "And don't we know that little Miss Kayla loves surprises. Well, I've got a surprise for you."

"Oh? What is it?" Kayla settled back on the futon. "And I hate to rush you, but you know I'm running."

Kayla laughed loudly as she listened to Amina's abridged version of a surprise date with Allen's brother Tim after he changed a flat tire on her Lexus. She always thought Amina and Tim had a thing for each other, even thought they had gone out a time or two, but neither ever seemed to be truly free. Either Amina was seeing someone or Tim was seeing someone. Now, according to Amina, they both were free.

"And that man is truly fine," Amina sang again. "Girl, and he's so romantic. I don't know why I wasted all my time with those other zeros when Tim is really the hero I've been waiting for."

The pair talked on for another fifteen minutes, with Kayla telling Amina about Allen knowing that Tim was their mechanic, and had been for some time. Amina quickly denied that she had told Tim anything at all about Kayla's love life, or lack thereof. Kayla wasn't so sure.

"But, girl, that Allen is one fine brother, too." Amina sang. "I'm going to let you go, but before I do, let me tell you something."

"Oh, God. Here comes a lecture." Kayla sighed.

"No, you're a grown woman. It's just a little sisterly advice. Don't run Kayla. No matter what does or does not happen, don't run from him. Enjoy this. It's not every day that two people get a second chance at love."

"I hear ya, Sister. Thanks."

"No problem. I've got to go myself. Tim and I are going to the DuSable Museum and then to lunch and then . . ." Amina began to snicker like a school girl. "Then, who knows."

"Have a good time, and tell Tim I said hello."

Kayla hung up, pushed the pause button on the stereo's remote, left the den and headed to her room. She pulled out a pair of olive colored jeans, a cream-colored turtle neck and her brown Lugz ankle boots. Allen had suggested she wear jeans and an overnight case. She showered, dressed, hung up the clothes that were strewn across her bed and floor, then made up her bed all in record time. The intercom rang.

"Who is it?" Kayla asked. No response. "Who is it?" she repeated. Still, no one answered. She turned her television on, selected the channel that would allow her to see the lobby. No one was there. She prayed it wasn't Jonathan and hoped like hell that it was someone who had pushed the wrong button. Moments later, when the buzzer sounded again, she was less pleasant.

"What?!" Kayla screamed into the intercom.

"Whoa." She heard Allen reply into the speaker. "It's just me."

"Come on up." She pressed the entry button, then grabbed her coat and purse. Kayla was ready for her surprise.

"Wow! Don't we look good today?" Allen smiled, then kissed Kayla lightly on the lips.

"Why thank you, but you know flattery will get you nowhere." She playfully chided then smiled, placing her overnight bag near the door.

"Dang, I thought I was gaining ground. Guess I'm going to have to resort to more desperate measures."

"Like what?" she asked, then wondered what more he could do.

Allen reached into the inside of the pocket of his black leather jacket and pulled out a long blue, faux velvet box. He handed it to Kayla and smiled as she gasped when she opened the box to reveal a stunning heart-shaped pendant, adorned with rubies and diamonds, and attached to a simple gold chain. He took the pendent from its place and delicately attached it around her slender neck.

"You have my heart," Allen said. He stepped closer, lessening the space between them, then kissed her full on the lips. The simple motion tumbled into a long, sensuous one that held a fiery intensity which surprised, yet delighted

Kayla. Allen had always been a thoughtful, gentle man in the past, but the passion, the searing message in his kiss, was something she had not experienced before.

Kayla kissed him back and draped her arms about his neck. The unobtrusive intention in their embrace, in their kiss, told all.

"Wooo, baby," Allen breathed. "The surprise isn't over. This is just the beginning. Are you ready to go?"

"Yes," Kayla kissed him again. "Where are we going?"

"You'll see." Allen winked, stole a look at his watch, motioned for her to grab her bag, then took her free hand in his. "This day belongs to us, baby. To us."

Chapter 12

Allen's hands covered Kayla's eyes. "No peeking." He whispered into her ear. "Just a few more steps."

She gasped when he removed his hands to reveal a black stretch limo. She looked up at Allen, who shrugged his shoulders, his foot patting the ground beneath them.

A chauffeur opened the door. Kayla, followed by Allen, sat inside, her body seduced by the plush leather seats and the warm interior.

"Driver," Allen began. "You know where to take us." Then he pushed the lever that raised the black tinted window secluding them from view. He picked up two champagne glasses from the wet bar in front of them.

"A toast," he filled their glasses. "To love lost and love found." He tapped her glass with his and sipped the gold liquid.

"Allen, what are you doing?" Kayla asked, her smile wide.

"You'll see," he replied, then removed her glass from her hand, setting hers next to his. He pulled her into his arms, his lips wet upon hers. She moaned deeply. "This will let you know how much I love you."

Kayla kissed him back, twisted her head slightly to the right and watched the city grow farther and farther away.

For nearly an hour, Allen teased and plied her. Roses. Champagne. Tender words of endearment. When the limo stopped, she looked up to see that they were at O'Hare Airport.

The chauffeur opened the door. Allen stepped out, then held his hand out for her to take. He pulled her into an embrace. "You might as well cancel any plans you had for today and tomorrow. We're going to spend the entire two days in the Bahamas."

Kayla was speechless as Allen led her across the tarmac to the waiting Leer jet. "Just relax and let me wait on you hand and foot. Your wish is my command."

Inside the private jet, Kayla gasped as she visually absorbed the plush surroundings. The ten forward facing seats, separated by two benches on both sides were upholstered in a warm steel grey plush velvet, the walls a beautiful shade of mauve.

Like a precocious child, she opened several standing compartments, eyeing the various wines and spirts they held before going to the next compartment which held several trays of fruit, vegetables and finger foods. Kayla looked at Allen and smiled. She had never been on a private jet.

"How did you manage this?"

"It belongs to one of my clients." He replied, ducking his head as he sat down. "We should be taking off in a minute. Come." He stretched out his hand. Kayla took it and sat next to him.

"Mr. Dawson and Miss Martin." The pilot appeared from the cockpit. "We have been cleared for take off. Please fasten your seat belts. When we are at a cruising altitude, feel free to move about the cabin. But keep your belts on if you remain in your seats."

"Thanks. We will." Allen looked at Kayla as the pilot closed the cabin door.

Once the jet achieved the determined altitude and the pilot's voice cracked over the intercom, Allen unfastened his seat belt, followed by Kayla's. He motioned for her to move to one of the row of benches.

She giggled, as Allen took off her boots, followed by her socks and began to rub her feet. All throughout the three and a half hour flight, Allen tended to her every imagined whim. Between heady kisses which left Kayla breathless, to the full body massage he gave her, Kayla was spellbound and more in love than she'd ever been.

Upon hearing the pilot was about to prepare for landing, they returned to their seats, their hands entwined, Kayla's thumb stroked across the flesh between Allen's thumb and index finger.

By the time they reached Paradise Island, she thought she would bust. Once inside their lavish suite, she walked to sliding glass doors which led to the private balcony. She gasped at the magnificent fifteenth floor view, which overlooked the aqua blue ocean and the crystal white beach below, green palm trees swaying in the warm Bahamian wind. She was at wit's end. All this was for her. A sudden emotion overtook her. She had to make love to him — had to feel his body upon hers, for she knew if he made love anything like he insinuated with his finger tips during that in-flight massage, she was going to lose her mind.

"Welcome to paradise, baby girl," Allen said then swept her off her feet suddenly. "Kayla, let me make love to you," he breathed and planted another kiss on her lips, this one with more fever than the first. "I've wanted to make love to you for so long."

Kayla nodded her head and allowed Allen to carry her to the bedroom.

She caught a brief glimpse of the massive king-sized bed situated in the middle of the room, a large whirlpool tub sat to the right.

Allen kissed her again, their tongues engaged in a tryst that neither wanted to end. She moaned. Her own fire was burning deep. Allen's lips left hers, leaving a trail across her face, around the top of her neck, then to the lobe of her ear. He blindly walked to the bedroom their unleashed passion was their guide, and placed her gently on the bed. He stood over her, the searing desire burned her to her core and she shivered from the anticipation that smoldered inside her. Slowly, Allen began to undress himself. He removed his long-sleeved shirt and undershirt. The dark satiny hairs lay smoothly on his well-formed chest. His male nipples hardened in the sudden cool air. Kayla watched him, her eyes following his hands as they moved to the belt secured around his waist. She could see he was straining to keep his composure, and she wanted to end his game, wanted to quickly remove what was left of his clothing. But the look on his face stood as a momentary delay to the fire she knew she would succumb to.

Allen lay next to Kayla and traced the outline of her face with his finger. She watched him as his thick hands skillfully moved over her body. She gasped when his fingers lingered long at the fabric which separated his hands from her breasts. He sat up, pulled Kayla to follow suit, then pulled her turtle neck over her head.

"Let me love you like only I can, Kayla," his voice was barely above a whisper as he reached around her back and unsnapped her bra, freeing her breasts from the flimsy white lace.

This time he stared at her. His eyes grew darker by the moment. Kayla watched the desire in them mount, and shivered loudly when she felt his tongue slip across a hardened nipple. She pulled his head closer and relished the longing his tongue had awakened.

Allen stopped and looked at her. He stood, took Kayla's hands in his and placed them on the buckle of his belt.

"Finish, please," he breathed.

Kayla's hands shook as she undid the buckle, followed by the snap on his jeans, then the zipper. She pushed the fabric down his hips and legs. He wrestled out of his shoes and socks before stepping out of his jeans. Kayla smiled slightly at the sight of Allen, nearly naked, his grey jockey briefs hugged his massive, muscular thighs and full member.

"You can touch me," Allen said and placed her hands on the band of his briefs. Kayla slowly rubbed her hands up his torso, letting her fingers splay in the silky smoothness of his hairy chest. She circled her fingers around his male nipples and smiled at their hardened response. Her fingers made their way back down his torso, pausing before making their way around him. She stroked him through the fabric, his head reared back, his eyes closed as she applied enough pressure to cause him to moan loudly.

He opened his eyes and stared down at Kayla as she massaged his hard member. He wasn't sure he could stand much more of her soft hands massaging him, feeling him. He almost lost all composure when she tugged at the fabric and freed him.

Kayla lay back and stared brazenly at Allen. It was almost as if she were seeing him for the first time, loving him for the first time. Her eyes drank in his handsome face, then slowly made their way down to his chest, across his flat stomach, then settled momentarily upon his thick member and finally to his beautifully muscular thighs. She blushed at her own boldness. She liked what she saw.

Allen put his hand out and pulled Kayla to stand on the floor. He removed her jeans and growled at the matching lace thong. When he had given her the body massage, he ignored the flimsy garment, not wanting to spoil this moment. Now he gave it its due attention, as he knelt in front of her and introduced his lips and tongue to the softness of her thighs. Kayla held onto his shoulders as the heat from his mouth threatened to send her into a whirling vortex. She gasped loudly as his oral search took him to the folds of her feminine being. His hands firmly held her full behind.

With his mouth, he kneaded, then rubbed — rubbed then kneaded her pearl. Kayla withered with each move, with each tortured touch from his hands and mouth. She tried to stop him, but his lips, followed by his tongue refused to obey and continued forward on their journey.

As she felt the beginning of her rise, Kayla undulated her hips forward. She couldn't help it. The pleasure she was receiving was like none she had ever experienced and she was loving every second of the rapture Allen's tongue and lips were bringing over and over.

She stiffened, closed her eyes, arched her back, then let out a brash shriek. The rise rumbled over her, held her in its fierce grasp. She sank slowly into its depth. Her long pent up desires cascaded. She had to have him.

Once the rumble subsided, she pulled Allen gently upward by his shoulders and moved slowly onto the bed until he lay atop her. She moved her hips up to meet his, then against him, her circular motions sent vicious chills up them both. But Allen had other thoughts, as he returned to making love to her entire body. He kissed, teased, and tongued Kayla up and down, and when she reached out to stop him, he gently held her hands to her sides and continued to let his mouth make love to her.

"Allen," Kayla gasped as another surge mounted. Her body tensed under his unrelenting movements. She held his head, letting the surge wash over her entire body once again.

Allen stealthily moved up her body, stopping to kiss and suck on her breasts.

Kayla wanted him. Wanted to feel him. She stretched out her arm and momentarily searched for her overnight case. It was nowhere to be found. She hated to break the spell.

"Umm, Allen, dear," she whispered.

Allen mumbled his response, his mouth full of one of her nipples.

"Baby, but we need protection."

Allen moved them toward the edge of the bed, his mouth fastened to her nipple, searched for his pants, then upon finding them, retrieved a foil package. Kayla took the package from his hand, tore it open, and wriggled from beneath him. She rolled the sheath over his throbbing member.

Kayla stared into Allen's eyes for a long moment. There was no turning back.

"I'm not going anywhere, Kayla." He stroked the side of her face. "I'm exactly where I want to be."

She laid her body onto his, allowing him to sink inside her depth. They were still — his arms like a vice around her. He didn't want to let her go.

He kissed her, his lips hot upon hers. She reeled in the taste of them, the softness. They began to move, together, placid, in unison. Kayla enjoyed the feel of him — wanted it to last a lifetime.

"Love me, Kayla. Let me feel it." Allen's voice was raspy.

She knew what he meant, knew he wanted to feel all of her, every part of her being, every inch of her soul.

Allen rolled them over, she beneath him, and entered her slowly. He began to move languidly within her, his senses whirling around him. He tried to control the threatening release, but found it more and more challenging when she wrapped her legs about his waist. The feel of her sweet, moist cavern, coupled with the feel of her arms around his back had him spinning. He wanted this feeling to last — to prolong the release.

Their lips matched their bodies in their torrid dance of passion and they both moaned loudly. His movements became immediate and Kayla matched them, thrusting her hips into his, then moving them in circles against him. He put his arms around her, held her tightly. Another surge threatened. This one stronger, more fervent. They both sensed it and allowed their bodies to mesh into one.

Tears streamed down Kayla's face as her passion mounted then took over. Her movements became more urgent as he sank deeper within her. She cried out as the surge mounted, then peaked. Allen followed. He allowed himself to feel her passion — her soul — the love he knew was for him and only him. He whispered his love in her ear as he reached his own release.

Allen continued to hold Kayla in his arms as he kissed her tears away and loved her like he wanted to, like she was meant to be loved. Totally. Completely. Without fear.

"I want you in my life forever, Kayla Martin," he said. "I want you forever. Can I have you with me always?"

Kayla didn't respond. She wanted to bask in the moment, in the passion and love Allen had awakened in her. Tomorrow wasn't what she wanted to think about. She knew she could love, was in love with the very man who at one time had made her heart stand still with the simple sound of his voice, a slight touch from his lips. Yet, this was also the very man who caused her world to collide. Still, here he was offering her an opportunity to finish what had been started, yet so abruptly interrupted years before. Kayla knew in her heart that this love, a second time around, was sweeter than before. The question became, could she accept it without fear.

Chapter 13

Allen stood at the foot of the deep ravine and let his eyes take in the massive pit. Large steel beams rose from it, making it look like fangs in a lion's mouth. He smiled from satisfaction as his mind conjured up the image of the great theater that would stand at this very location in just ten short months. Built to resemble a grand old movie house from the 1920's, Allen had designed the outside of the theater with white Terra Cotta, laced with intricate carvings of Greek gods from one end to the other. Inside, the theater would house three thousand seats, with several levels, all with unobstructed views of two stages, one stacked upon the other, below. Large columns, braced in the four corners of the theater, would also resemble those found among the ruins in Greece. This, he mused, was undoubtedly his most creative, yet challenging design to date.

He had hired the best. The best tradesmen and construction workers in North America. No expense would be too great. And because of his sound decision, the project was six months ahead of schedule. This, he knew, would result in a nice financial award.

He walked over to the makeshift table, a wooden ply-board set upon a construction horse. He studied the second phase of construction and called to the site foreman.

"Bill," Allen began. "These retaining walls have to be thicker."

"It's up to code," Bill responded, tersely. Allen thought he detected a hint of animosity in his voice. He knew that Bill was the best concrete man in the construction business, which was the reason he hired him. But he also knew that he had come from a long line of men who believed that African-Americans couldn't design, much less possess any knowledge of what it took to construct a building. Allen watched the man's face turn a deep crimson.

"Listen," he stepped closer. The last thing he wanted was a scene. "I don't give a damn about being up to code. I want it to surpass code. Got me?" Allen refused to be put off. His summers had been spent working in construction, first in high school, then in college. He knew every facet of construction. If he wanted, he could build a house with his bare hands. "I want the wall thicker." Allen turned his attention back to his drawings. He spied the foreman's work boots from the corner of his eye, then looked up into the man's steel grey eyes. "Is there anything else?" The man shook his head, then walked away.

Allen rolled his eyes upward. Just ten more months, he said to himself. Suddenly his attention was drawn by the sound of his name being called. "Hey, Dawson. You got a visitor."

He turned to see Kayla walking toward him, a white hard hat haplessly placed on her head, a wicker picnic basket held by her side. He smiled.

"What are you doing here?" he asked. Pulling her into his arms, he kissed her. She blushed at the sounds of whistles and whoops from the workers.

"I wanted to see you in action," she looked up at him, then let her eyes sweep across his chamois colored work boots, form fitting jeans, denim shirt and brown leather jacket. Kayla knew he couldn't be more handsome. She grinned as Allen righted the hard hat upon her head. "You've already seen me in action. Want to see me in action again?" The seduction in his voice caused Kayla to shiver. She playfully swatted his arm. "You are so bad."

"Only for you, baby girl." He reluctantly released her, then nodded his head at the basket. "Wha' cha got there?"

"I figured you hadn't eaten lunch. And since I'm free for at least two hours," she smiled up at him, "I figured we'd eat lunch together."

"Here?"

"Why not?" Kayla looked around and scrunched up her nose. "Well, maybe not here. How about over at Grant Park?"

"Now, that sounds like a plan," Allen agreed, then pulled a set of keys from his pocket. "Why don't you go get the car? It's parked around the back. I'll meet you there in fifteen minutes." He kissed her on her nose, then turned her body and gave her a gentle push. He shifted his attention to the drawings.

Fifteen minutes turned into an hour, as Kayla sat in the car waiting for Allen to join her. She was becoming more and more impatient, turning the dials on the radio and playing with the various features on her cell phone. To say she was agitated was putting it mildly, but her agitation waned when she looked up to see Allen hastening toward the car, his jeans hugging him in all the right places. She couldn't help the wicked smile which splayed across her face.

"I'm so sorry, baby," he began, then kissed her quickly. "There was a slight problem. How much time do we have left?"

"About an hour."

"Then I know a special place. You game?"

Kayla nodded. She watched him as he put the car in gear and pulled out of the makeshift parking spot behind the construction site.

Allen hummed along with the radio, his eyes stealing glances at Kayla every few seconds. From the looks of him, she could tell he was up to something, but didn't dare ask. When they pulled into another construction site, her curiosity got the best of her.

"Don't tell me. Another building you have to check on."

"Nope. Sit tight." He parked, grabbed the picnic lunch from the backseat, retrieved a blanket from the trunk, then came to the passenger side and helped Kayla from the car. He led her to an open hoist, placed a hard hat on her head, then one on his own, pulled the safety bar across the hoist, then pushed a red button. Kayla was startled by the sudden jerk, then chug of the open-air contraption. She held onto Allen's arm. "Now, that's more like it," he said, then put his arm around her shoulder.

Kayla's eyes widened as the city scape crept into view, the magnificent skyline looked close enough to touch. She inched closer to Allen as they jerked to a halt.

Removing the safety bar, Allen stepped out of the hoist, then took her hand in his, and began to walk across the large concrete floor. At a wooden door, he jiggled the lock, then pushed it open. Kayla gasped at the sight in front of her. Floor to ceiling windows all around her were accented by a thick plush carpet of pure white, the walls painted an even starker white. She looked at the exquisite wall sconces of pewter, and walked slowly toward one of the large windows. "Allen, this is beautiful. You designed this?"

"Yup," he responded. "Personally," he ended with a hint of pride in his voice.

"I'm impressed. What is the building going to be, when its finished?" she asked.

"When its finished, the whole building is going to be condos," he began. "This is the penthouse. The owner specifically requested these types of windows and they're quite expensive and tempered to withstand anything Chicago's weather can conjure up. Plus, you can see out, but no one can see in."

Kayla walked to within inches from the window, the city several stories below. At every angle, she had an unobstructed view of Chicago and Lake Michigan. "Imagine the simple beauty of this at night," she said. "It must cost a mint."

"Sure does. How does two-point-one-million sound to you?"

"Sounds too rich for my blood."

Allen stood behind her, his arms wrapped around her. "Umm, would I love to be up here at night." He turned her to face him. "With you." He bent to reach her lips, her mouth opened slightly to accept his. They moaned, the lunch forgotten as their passion enveloped them.

Allen broke the embrace only long enough to place the blanket on the carpeted floor. He sat, and stretched his arms out toward her. Basking in his embrace, emotions swirling around her, she knew her reservations about him were melting. Their two-day visit to Paradise Island just two weeks before had connected them as never before. They had sunbathed on the warm sand during the day in swimsuits bought on the island. And made love at every conceivable spot, every chance they got. On the balcony. At a secluded spot on the beach. In the in-room whirlpool Jacuzzi tub. As the sun rose, and as the sun set. It was as if neither could get enough of the other.

Brought back to the present, Kayla heard Allen's voice as it stole into her being — its depth, and deep richness resonated around her, comforting her. "Baby girl, I'm going to love you a thousand lifetimes," he said, and began to undress her, then followed by himself. She wrapped him in her arms and let him love her languidly and long.

Satiated, Allen's head against her chest, the rhythm of her heartbeat threatened to lull him to sleep, the vibrations soft against his cheek. He smiled as her hand stroked the side of his face, her touch tender and full of love. The words, though, hadn't come and he felt a twinge in his heart. Maybe she didn't love him, he thought, then quickly pushed the damning reverb away. It's okay, he mused; he felt he had enough love for the both of them. He raised his head, then looked into her eyes.

"We forgot about lunch," he laughed.

Kayla blushed. "That we did. But you're a perfect substitute."

He kissed her right breast, before taking the areola fully into his mouth. His right eyebrow rose at the sound of Kayla's moan.

"And if you keep that up, we'll be here all night," she breathed.

"Ummm," he began, reluctantly releasing the erotic hold. "Now, would that be so bad?" He looked up at her. "Guess not," he replied to her silence, then rolled over onto his back, protected them with a latex sheath, then pulled her on top of him. When he felt her warm cavern enclose him, her resplendent movements eliciting deep, involuntary moans from him, he knew he could never get enough of her. And though she hadn't told him that she loved him, he knew that he couldn't go back to yesterday. Wouldn't go back to a life without her. He knew there was only one thing to do. But would she have him?

Chapter 14

Kayla and Allen had settled into loving each other — almost as if they had never been apart. For weeks, thereafter, Allen kept up his attentiveness, providing surprise lunches at her office, dinners, plays and late nights of videos. Their love had become a part of their lives, almost as if they had never been separated. Kayla relished the feelings she was experiencing, even on those occasions when she would become frightened of her emotions; uncertain that the feelings she was experiencing were real. But Allen would always soothe her with his simple phrase of "I'm not going anywhere, Kayla."

Her heart had thawed. And with it, came a new resolve. She would love Allen for as long as he would allow her to and would continue to fight the niggling voice of fear. Her only problem now was Jonathan. Though she had told Allen all about her marriage to Jonathan, she hadn't told him of the continued phone calls she was receiving from him no less than six times daily. She felt slightly odd not telling Allen that he was stalking her, and that she had seen him sitting in his car across from her loft when they had returned from one of their outings. She thought she could handle him alone. Besides, if Allen had interfered, for sure, things would get worse, not better. No, for once, she felt she had to navigate the whole situation on her own, without anyone's assistance. She knew this was a solo act.

Formerly, she had felt Jonathan's calls were more of a nuisance than anything else. What was disturbing now, however, was the fact that whenever Allen was at her loft, the phone would ring several times, she would answer, but there would be no one on the other end. Her caller ID showed private each time. At work, she would also get the same type of calls. It was beginning to unnerve her. She knew it wasn't Jonathan. He always spoke. Though nothing he said ever made any sense, at least she knew who it was. She forced her mind back on her work, preparing final exams for her class. The intercom on her desk phone rang.

"Kayla, its Mr. Dawson on line one."

"Thanks Linda," she replied and picked up the receiver.

"Hey beautiful." Allen's voice seeped out.

"How are you today?"

"Thinking of you. What are you doing tonight?"

Kayla looked over her desk. She saw a pair of feet standing at the door. She figured only she and Linda were in the office. Why would she be standing outside my door? She wondered.

"Kayla? You still there?" Allen asked.

"Yeah, sorry. What did you say?"

"What are you doing tonight?"

"Nothing. What are you doing tonight?"

"Aside from trying to be with you, beautiful, I'm going to head to the gym, then have a little dinner with you. That is, if you don't mind?" he replied.

She smiled. Yeah, she thought — she wanted to be with him. She wanted to be with him every chance she got.

The feet moved from the door. Kayla made a mental note to address the issue the next time it occurred.

"You know I don't mind," she replied. "What do you want to do? I'm in the middle of creating the final exams for my classes. I'm nowhere near finished, but I can be ready to go after six."

"How about some dinner at The Village?"

"That sounds great, Allen. What time?"

"About six-thirty? It's two now, so that should give you enough time to finish up."

"Okay, Allen. See you at six-thirty."

"That's beginning to seem like a long time . . . "

Kayla didn't respond. The feet had returned to her door. She stood up, placed the phone down, tipped over to the door, then opened it quickly.

"Can I help you?" Kayla demanded as she stared at the attractive woman standing in front of her. She looked past the woman's shoulder, searching for Linda. "Umm, do you have an appointment?" The woman stared at her. Kayla was taken aback at the hate she saw blazing in the woman's eyes. "I mean, is there something I can help you with?"

"Well, no Professor Martin," the woman began, sweeping her dark brown, shoulder length hair with one finger behind her ear. "I just wanted to stop in to see what all the fuss was about."

"Fuss?"

"Yes." The woman's mahogany eyes never left Kayla's, her voice came out low and raspy. "You seem to be a big hit."

Kayla's face became a mask of uncertainty. Now on guard, she was wishing that Linda was sitting at her desk. The woman standing in front of her seemed maniacal, unstable and Kayla couldn't stop staring into her eyes. Her thoughts were interrupted. "I mean, your students seem to really enjoy your class." The woman corrected.

"Thank you. Are you interested in the writing program?" The woman nodded her head. "Well, when the receptionist returns, I'll have her get your name and address, and give you some information on the program."

"That will be fine. I'll just sit here and wait."

A deep fear rose in Kayla's chest as she watched the woman sit in the chair across from Linda's desk. She smiled at her, and the woman smiled back, though it never reached her eyes. Kayla closed the door. She had never seen venom this close and directed at her. She wondered who the woman was. Quickly she opened the door again. The woman was gone. She stepped out in the reception area and looked around before heading back to her office. She shut the door, locked it, then picked up the phone.

"Kayla, what's going on?"

She hesitated. How could she tell Allen that she had feared a nameless woman? She decided against telling him.

"Oh, nothing to be concerned about. Just someone interested in the program. I'll see you later?"

"Yes, Baby. I can't wait."

She hung up, but she couldn't shake the spooky feelings the woman roused in her. She knew there was something, but she just couldn't put her finger on it.

For over two hours, Kayla tried to complete the task of grading papers. The raspy voice now embedded in her mind. She shook her head, trying to loosen the fear that had gripped her. Upon hearing footsteps again, she ran to the door. "Linda?!" Kayla began. "Some strange woman was here. Did you see her?"

"No, I went to lunch. And when I got back, I had a note on my desk that the Dean wanted to see me. What happened?"

Kayla realized the panic in her voice. "Nothing. She was just strange, that's all."

"I meant to tell you I was going to be away from my desk," Linda replied, then tilted her head to the right. "Wait. I went to the Dean's office and waited for nearly an hour. When she arrived, she said she didn't need me."

"That's odd."

"Did you get a good look at her?"

"Well, she had long dark hair and a pair of creepy eyes. But her voice was so eerie. Like something out of Creature Feature."

"I think we need to call the guard." She reached for the phone.

"No, don't do that," Kayla said, placing her hand on Linda's. "She was probably just one of the students. But you can do me a favor." Linda nodded. "Next time just slip a note under my door telling me you're leaving."

"Will do."

Kayla returned to her office, leaving the door open. Looking at the clock on her desk, she realized she had only two hours to finish creating the final exam. She forced the image of the mahogany eyes from her mind and went back to her work.

After several hours, Kayla gathered her things to leave. "I'm about to head out. I'll see you on Monday."

"Have a wonderful weekend, Kayla. And tell Mr. Dawson I said hello."

"I will. You too," she said, waving goodbye. She stopped at the Dean's office, then headed to the elevator. The more Kayla thought about it, the more disturbed she became at the strange phone calls she had been receiving over the past couple of months; both at home and at work. And though the woman had only stared at her, something inside of her wouldn't let the venom in the woman's eyes disappear. Kayla hadn't gotten a good mental picture of her face, but the woman's voice she would recognize anywhere.

Allen grabbed his wide gym bag, then headed out to his car. He took his cell phone from the middle console and dialed his buddy, Mike.

"You ready?" Allen started up the car.

"Yeah, I'll meet you there."

Allen depressed the end button, replaced the cell phone, and moved into the light traffic. His mind careened carelessly in and out, thoughts of Bahamas and Kayla intertwined throughout. She was still solidly in his thoughts as he pulled up in front of the glass encased health club, parked, then headed inside. He spied Mike standing at the reception desk.

"What's up, my brother?" Mike gripped Allen's hand, then embraced him. "You're looking awfully happy. What's up?" He stepped back and looked into Allen's eyes.

"Nothing," Allen averted the gaze, but couldn't stifle the slight chuckle that escaped. "Let's get this workout in. I've got an appointment at 6:30."

Mike followed Allen, his attention momentarily snatched by a woman standing near the rows of step machines. He knew her. The realization snapped. It was Keisha, one of Allen's old flames.

"Hey, man," Mike bent to whisper. "There's a blast from the past here."

Allen's eyes followed Mike's, landing on the last person he thought he would ever see. Though he had not been cold, he had been firm with Keisha when he told her he no longer wanted to see her. He thought he was doing the right thing, telling her the truth about his inability to commit. Allen cringed as he watched Keisha walk toward them. A low whistle escaped from Mike and he knew just what his boyhood friend was thinking. Still, a beautiful face and a slam-ming body didn't make the woman.

"Hey Mike," Keisha came to stand before them. "Hi, Allen. Long time no see."

"Yeah, Keisha. How've you been?"

"I'm faring. How about you? How's Daniel?" She swept her long hair behind her ear.

"We're both doing fine."

Silence gripped the trio as Mike looked from Allen to Keisha, then back to Allen. He knew that Keisha was the last person he ever wanted to run into, especially after her scene at his home following their breakup. For Allen, who had tried to avoid drama at all costs, especially after the hurt he caused Kayla, Keisha's pleading and crying made him regret ever having gone out with her. He could have kicked him-self. Daniel had always stayed his distance whenever Keisha came to visit, and he should have been more attuned to his son's behavior. At least with Sharon, Daniel had sat on the stairs and watched her.

"Well, Keisha," Allen began. "It was good seeing you. Gotta go." He walked quickly toward the locker rooms, put on his sweats, then headed out. As they stepped out onto the floor, Keisha was still near the stair machines, openly staring at him. A slight sweat broke out across Allen's forehead. He didn't like what he saw flashing in her eyes.

Allen and Mike chatted between sets of lifting weights, doing crunches, and pushups, heavy banter over who was the strongest filled each area they visited. After an hour of working out, they showered, dressed, then headed out of the club.

"Man, what's up with her?" Mike pointed with his thumb over his shoulder. "Everywhere we went in that club, that chick was there."

"I don't know and I really don't want to." Allen looked at his watch. "Hey, I gotta jet. I'm picking up . . ."

Mike stepped in front of Allen. "Ahh-ha. I knew it." A large grin appeared on his boyish, round face. "I knew it. You got a new lady. Okay, gimme the skinny. Who is she?"

Allen slowly walked to the rear of his car, opened the truck, placed his bag inside, then peered over the top before shutting it. "Mike, you are so nosey," he said as he made his way to the driver's side. He knew he was driving Mike crazy by stalling. Yet, he wasn't sure he was ready to admit that he had been right, that it was partially his words which made him realize that he had and would always love Kayla.

"Allen!" Mike snapped. "Come on man!"

Allen laughed. "All right. I'm seeing Kayla, again."

"Yeah, boy!" Mike placed his hand in the air for a high-five. "I always liked that girl. How's she doing? She still look the same? Fine as ever"

"She's well. Divorced. No kids. And all mine." Allen winked, climbed in the car, then started it up. As he placed the car in reverse, he poked his head out of the window. "And I'm going to ask her to marry me." He spun out of the lot. Looking in the rear view mirror, he laughed upon seeing the shocked expression plastered on Mike's face. His smile quickly faded as Keisha's image appeared next to Mike.

Chapter 15

A wide grin spread across Kayla's face as she strolled out into the warm sun and into Allen's arms.

"Let's walk," he said and took her by the hand.

They walked along Michigan Avenue. The warm May evening had brought scores of people out. The Art Institute's stark white steps were crowded with people ogling the street vendors performing musical acts. Allen pulled her close, placing a kiss on her forehead.

"Umm, that was nice," Kayla purred. "You're in a good mood today. Work must be going great."

"Not only that, but you Kayla." Allen stopped them. "You are what's going great for me. I had never known real love, Kayla, until you loved me. Then I went and threw it away out of fear."

Kayla stroked the side of his face, then placed her index finger upon his lips. "Allen, that was yesterday. Let's just live for today."

"I just want you to know that I love you Kayla. That's all."

She stood on the tips of her toes, kissed Allen sweetly on the lips, then entwined her arm through his.

Several blocks later, they arrived at the restaurant. Kayla had always liked his choice of restaurants, especially this one. The quaint old world feel was one of the many qualities she liked about the Italian Village Restaurants.

"I knew you would like this," he said as he opened the door.

"It's been years since I've eaten here."

"Me too," he replied as he took her hand and led her up the stairs to The Village.

Oil paintings of Venice and Milan hung on the deep, oak walls. Kayla glanced up at the ceiling of painted stars complemented by a bright full moon.

Each table in the restaurant was set with small votive candles atop stark white table cloths. The maitre d' escorted them to their seats, a private booth in the rear. Allen ordered a bottle of vino before shutting the door to the booth.

They fell easily into conversation, neither hurried nor forced. Kayla spoke of her plans for the summer. Allen spoke of things he and Daniel would do during that same time. Each watched the other, attempting to read the thoughts that floated in and out of their minds. As on cue, they both spoke.

"What are you going to order?" they chimed in unison, then smiled at one another. Allen covered her hands resting upon the table, then said, "I guess great minds think alike."

She nodded, absently stroking the heart-shaped pendant around her neck. What she really wanted to say was that she had fallen in love with him — again. He had told her how he felt, how much he loved her, but she had yet to tell him of her feelings, even though he seemed to wash away her every fear with a kiss, or a word, or a look. Allen always seemed to know what she needed, wanted.

A knock on the door signaled the return of the maitre d'. Allen ordered Salmone con Salsa di Gaspacho, and Kayla ordered the Costolette di Vitello alla Griglia.

Throughout dinner they talked and laughed — the ten years they spent apart were now mere days. Kayla wanted to end the night on a special note. It was more than time for her to admit to Allen her true feelings, but she wanted to do so in a manner he wouldn't ever forget, much like he had done.

Allen looked at her. "Hey, a penny for your thoughts."

"A nickel for a kiss," Kayla began to sing. "A dime if you tell me that you love me."

Allen chuckled. "You remember that song?"

"How could I forget it. You sang it to me each and every day."

They laughed easily.

"I want to do something special for you tonight. Will you let me, Allen?"

"Baby, you can do anything you want for me." Allen's eyes narrowed, the sensuality in them clear. "What do you have in mind?"

"Let me take a cab home, then come over in two hours."

"Take a cab?" he began to protest.

Kayla covered his hands with hers. "Trust me." She leaned over and kissed him, lightly at first, then traced the outline of his lips with her tongue, followed by short nibbles. She then suckled his bottom lip, teasing him, darting her tongue in and out of his mouth. Her fingers roamed across his face, then down his chest, stopping just at the band of his slacks. She heard him moan.

"Woman," Allen breathed.

"Yes, man," she replied coyly.

"What are you trying to do to me?"

"Come over in two hours and I will show you."

They left the restaurant, with Allen hailing her a cab. "What am I going to do for two hours?" He pouted.

Kayla poked her head through the window, pulled his face closer, and kissed him quickly. As the cab pulled away, she called back to him. "You'll find something to do."

She waved goodbye and blew him a kiss. Allen stood there with his hands in his pockets.

The buzz from the intercom announced his arrival. Kayla stole one last glance at herself in the bedroom mirror, looked around her loft, and opened the door.

"Oh my," Allen breathed out. "Umph, umph, umph."

"Come in Mr. Dawson." She swept her arm around his waist, almost pulling him across the threshold. "Would you care for some champagne?"

"Umm, I.. umm, yeah."

Kayla smiled wickedly. She wasn't disappointed in the effect her short, sheer black chemise and its matching robe was having on Allen. She purposely left the robe open. "Follow me." She took his hand in hers. This wasn't the Bahamas, but she was determined to make it paradise for him.

Allen obeyed, watching the vicious sway of her hips; the simple movements made him want to grab her and make love to her right then and there. He fought to restrain himself, knowing she had gone to great lengths to prepare her surprise for him. Just for him.

They stopped at the bathroom door.

"Baby, I want you to go in there, undress and climb in," she whispered, her eyes full of promise. "I'll join you momentarily."

All Allen could do was nod, as Kayla walked away. Her robe moving fluidly from side to side before she disappeared toward the kitchen.

Allen opened the door and gasped. The entire bathroom was lit with candles. Candles set atop the vanity, all along the tops of the whirlpool tub and the window sill. Candles even lit a path to the tub. He smiled, when strings introduced the first song on "Barry White's Greatest Hits." Never had Allen experienced anything like this. He was both shocked and impressed. "Baby has it in her after all," he whispered.

He undressed, put his big toe into the water, then climbed in. The jets of the tub swirled warm water around him. Allen laid his head on the inflatable pillow and closed his eyes, his imagination running wild.

"Baby, are you in the tub?" Kayla asked as she pushed open the door.

Allen opened his eyes slowly, taking in the beauty of Kayla's face as she stood near the door holding a tray.

"What do you have there?"

Kayla raised one eyebrow. "You'll see."

She walked over to the small vanity, placed the tray atop it, picked up the two fluted glasses full of champagne and strolled over to stand close to the tub.

Allen took the glasses from her and set them on a nearby shelf. "Why don't you join me?" It was more a gentle order than a request.

Kayla nodded, slowly pushing the robe down her shoulders, letting the garment fall to the floor. Her eyes never left his, as she pushed the thin straps of the chemise down across her arms, then down her hips, her nakedness highlighted by the candles.

"Kayla, you are so beautiful." Allen held out his hand. She took it and stepped into the tub, then leaned over to press her body close to his.

She placed her finger over his lips as he began to speak. "Tonight, my love, I will do all the talking for both of us." She smiled when Allen acquiesced.

Kayla picked up the champagne glass, placed it to his lips and watched as he sipped. She then took a loofa scrub and began to gently wash him, beginning with his arms, followed

by his chest. When she moved to the opposite end of the
large tub, she reached under the water and lifted his foot,
gently massaging the soles, letting her hand travel up his
large calf, then his muscular thigh. She stopped at his growing member. She had other plans for that.

Kayla returned to his side, took his hands in hers, soaped
them, then placed them on her full breasts, guiding them in
slow, deliberate circles. When she heard him groan, she
moved his hands down her stomach, to the curly hairs that
hid her pearl. Her eyes never left his, as she guided him. His
fingers wreaked their own sweet havoc on her senses. She
moaned lightly, then began to wash him, paying special
attention to his fully engorged member.

"Baby," he began. "I'm loving every minute of this."

"Shhh," she chided lightly. "This is only the beginning."

He wondered what else could she do. His curiosity did-
n't last long. Kayla stepped out of the tub, seized a towel and
opened her arms to him.

Allen followed, coming to her. She patted him dry, dried
herself, then led him by the hand to her bedroom. She
motioned for him to lie on the bed, then disappeared. She
returned with the tray and Allen could see several vials of oil
arranged atop it.

"Pick your oil, darling," she ordered. Allen chose the
musk. Kayla knelt on the bed, picked up the vial, and
dripped it over his body. Slowly she massaged him, beginning with his arms, followed by his chest, down his torso,
across his legs, then onto his feet. "Roll over."

Allen obeyed, and was quickly rewarded with the feel of her soft, delicate hands gliding smoothly up and down his entire back. He shivered when her hands were replaced with her body, as she expertly slid her entire body up and down his.

"Roll over again."

He complied. Kayla repeated the ministrations, rubbing her breasts up and down his entire body. He was hot with passion, with need, as he felt her hand envelope his member. He wasn't sure he could hold back. She was driving him mad with her seduction, yet he loved every agonizing moment.

His eyes rolled inside his head when he felt the wetness of her lips take him in. The slow movements, followed by the tightening of her lips sent him into ecstasy. He was lost. His need burned deep and slow.

"Woman, what are you doing to me?" he hoarsely demanded. "Baby, you are driving me crazy."

His words only made Kayla more determined. She exerted more pressure, feeling his hands wander blindly through her hair. The more she moved her lips, the louder he moaned. When she touched the sacks which held his seed, he shuddered, his behind rose from the bed. She placed her free hand on his stomach, gently pushing him downward as she continued to let her mouth make love to him.

Without warning, Allen grabbed Kayla by her shoulders and pulled her from him. "I've got to have you," he breathed. "I don't want to wait any longer."

Kayla pursed her lips. She stealthily moved her body over his, positioning herself over his rock hard member.

"Are you sure?" She teased.

"Yes," he replied, almost begged.

She slowly slid upon him, and the entry made them both shiver. Kayla moved her hips, twirling them, extracting the pleasure she knew they both needed. She quickened her gyrations, his words of love and need encouraging her onward. Then she felt it, her own release building. Kayla had always insisted on protection, but she threw caution to the wind as her own passion took control. She was lost in the thirst for love.

Allen surprised her, when he moved her from atop him, had her on all fours, and entered her. She was insane with passion, as she felt his hardness move fluidly inside of her. But this was her seduction, and she reluctantly moved away from him and lay on her back, her arms outstretched, her legs just as wide. She stroked her hair and motioned for him to come to her.

He came to her, sinking inside her cavern yet again. He stilled himself, not wanting this love she was giving him to be over too soon. Yet when she started moving her hips against his, he couldn't contain it. He had to have the release, had to fill her with his love. He looked into her eyes — the love and passion mixed with naked lust was plain to see.

"Allen, I love you," Kayla said returning his stare.

"Say that again, please." He wanted to hear it. He needed to hear her say the words he had longed to hear come from her lips and only her lips.

"Allen, yes, I love you. I love you so much."

He sank further. They moved together, the need rising hot and furious. With every stroke, she met him, exceeded him, joined him. And upon sensing her release, the tightening of her cavern was his signal and he thrust deeper inside her, until he heard her cry out his name, the sound of her voice like sweet nectar to his very soul. Upon the very sound of his name, he allowed his own release, filling Kayla with all that he had — hoping she knew that she was all that he would ever need.

Following, he cradled her in his arms. A single tear fell from the corner of his eye. She rose to kiss him, lightly stroking his face, then snuggled back into his arms. Allen knew, at that moment, no matter what, that they would be together always. This love — their love would never be finished.

Chapter 16

Allen squinched his eyes against the imposing rays of the daylight streaming through the blinds. He glanced at Kayla sleeping beside him, her back to him. This was what he wanted. He wanted her in his arms and in his bed each and every day and night of his life. He shook her gently.

"Good morning, beautiful."

Kayla looked up, stretched her arms, then covered her mouth as she yawned. "Good morning to you. I take it from the grin on your face, that you had a wonderful night."

"Umm, I did," Allen replied, his member stirred reminding him of the love-filled passion shared with her. She scooted closer to him, placing her backside against his crotch and began rotating slowly. "Baby, you better stop that, or else we won't get out of this bed today."

Kayla quickened her movements. "You sure?" she replied seductively, turning to face him.

Allen groaned, then forced himself to think other thoughts, for today he wanted her to meet Daniel.

"Kayla, I think it's time you met my little man."

She blinked. She had already been to his house. Allen had told her all about its poor condition when he first purchased it. And she felt the pride in his voice, saw it etched across his handsome face when he showed her the imposing three-story greystone from top to bottom.

Allen led her around his home. From his home office, painted a deep charcoal grey, surrounded by an art decco border near the ceiling, to Daniel's room which was painted a bold red and white, with life-sized Super Hero characters painted on each of the four walls. When he stopped at his bedroom, decorated in deep mahogany and green, with specks of gold dotted in borders, his comforter and area rug, she could see the longing in his eyes. They both smiled at the large poster bed.

He had ended the tour with the kitchen. Kayla pictured herself there, cooking meals for Allen and Daniel in the massive kitchen. She had always wanted a large kitchen. Had always wanted a family to fuss over, see after, love. Yes, she thought, she could see herself living in this house, and taking care of the man she loved.

Kayla came back to the present and nodded her head in agreement.

"Baby, let's get dressed and head over to the house." Allen kissed her on the lips, then rose from the bed. He looked down at her. She had never looked more beautiful, lying there, her hair tousled sexily about her head, her nipples hard.

"Ah, how about we take a few moments?" Allen smiled, returning to the bed. "A man could become quite spoiled."

"Baby," Kayla began. "Not any man." She opened her arms. "This man." She pointed her index finger lightly into Allen's chest, as he came to her once again.

A pensive look was plastered on Kayla's face as they exited the expressway leading to Allen's home.

"What is it, baby?"

"I'm nervous."

"Why? Daniel's going to love you."

"It's just nerves. I'll be okay." Kayla dismissed her feelings. She felt honored that he had wanted her to meet his son, the child she knew he loved with all his heart.

Allen helped Kayla out of the car and together they walked toward the door of his house. There stood Daniel standing beside Yolanda. His face was pleasant, but his eyes were cast downward.

"Yolanda, you remember Kayla?"

"Yes, its nice to see you again. It's been a long time." She took Kayla's hands in hers. "Allen told me you teach at East-West and that you've written a book. I've never met an author."

"Neither had I until my book came out." Kayla joked. "As for East-West, its great. Actually I really like teaching and the semester is almost over, so I'll have the whole summer to myself."

"Must be nice," Yolanda replied.

Allen put his hand out toward Daniel. Daniel stood near his aunt, his hand gripped around hers. Yolanda looked at Kayla, then to Allen, then down to Daniel.

"Little man," Allen began. "I want you to meet Kayla. Remember I told you about her."

Daniel nodded but remained by his aunt's side. Allen eyed Yolanda.

"Daniel, sir. Look at me," Allen said softly, yet firmly. They all watched as the little boy lifted his head and looked at his father. "Can you at least speak to our guest?"

Daniel nodded his head, looked up at Kayla, then ran away. Allen started after him, but Yolanda stopped him. "Allen, let me handle this."

Kayla was taken aback. "He's shy?"

"Not at all," replied Allen. "I don't know what's wrong."

Kayla and Allen waited a moment, then went on inside the house. Shortly thereafter, Yolanda reappeared.

"Allen can I talk to you for a minute?" she asked.

Kayla could hear the hushed tones between them in the kitchen. She was nervous, anxious. She sat on the sofa and looked around the room. A movement to her left caught her eye. There was Daniel sitting on the steps watching her. She smiled. He only looked. She waved. He continued to stare. His eyes seemed to soak her in. When she rose to stand at the bottom of the stairs, Daniel ran up them toward his room.

Moments later, Allen and Yolanda returned to the room. Yolanda went upstairs and returned with a bag and Daniel in tow. Allen walked over to Daniel, lifted him in his arms, kissed him on the cheek. "I love you, Daniel."

Daniel nodded and left with his aunt.

"What's the matter?" Kayla inquired.

"He's afraid."

"Of me?!"

"No, of getting close to you. He told Yolanda that if he liked you, got to know you, then you would leave."

"My God, Allen, where'd he get that notion from?"

"I'm afraid from me. I never had a chance to tell him what happened with Sharon and Keisha. And he really liked Sharon. He thinks her leaving is his fault."

"Wow. That's heavy. What do you want me to do? I mean, what can we do to ease his fears?"

"You can say yes to marrying me."

Kayla froze. Sure she loved Allen, she had said it, felt it. And she wanted to be with him night and day, even saw herself as queen of Allen's castle, but marry him? Marry again? Fear rose in her throat. She couldn't think. Her mind became thick with wild images of Allen falling out of love with her, of his leaving her again. There was no way she was going to marry again, only to have her love thrown in her face. She was sure that the pain she once felt would consume her so much that she wouldn't be able to stand it a second time.

Yet she had to be honest with herself, for she knew this time around was different. This was exactly what she wanted, had wanted ten years ago. They were two different people now. Still, she wanted to be sure, for the niggling voice was doing battle with the logical one.

Allen watched the fear in her eyes quickly replaced by questioning, then resolve. He sighed a breath of relief.

"I love you, Kayla and I want to be with you now and forever." He knelt in front of her, then reached into his pocket. "I want to sleep with you in my arms. I want to roll over and make love to you in the middle of the night. I want you here, with me and Daniel."

Kayla looked at Allen, the love and sincerity that shone in his eyes were unmistakable.

She quieted the niggling voice. "Allen, what do you want me to say?" A single tear fell down her cheek.

"Say yes."

Kayla closed her eyes, trying to steady her heart and her head. This is it, she told herself. When she opened her eyes, Allen was still there, his hand in hers, the black velvet box in the other. He removed the ring from its box, removed her "never getting married ring," from her finger, and replaced it with a sparkling pear-shaped ruby marquis, surrounded by diamond baguettes.

"Yes, Allen. Yes." She cried as she pulled him upward into an embrace. "Yes, I'll marry you."

Chapter 17

"So, how have your dates with Allen been?" Laura quizzed. "Have you fallen yet?"

Kayla sat up straight in her bed. She rubbed her eyes and focused on her sister as she stood at the foot of her bed.

"You heard me!" Laura snapped. "You've been seeing him for months now. Why the secrets, Kayla?!"

She slid from under the covers and headed to the bathroom. She wondered how Laura found out, but before she could ask, Laura barged into the bathroom.

"Can I have a little privacy? Please?!" Kayla asked.

"Hell, no! I want to know why you've been going out with Allen Dawson, of all people?"

"Because he asked me to," she responded snidely.

"Don't get cute, Kayla. Remember, he's the one who broke your heart and then left for no reason. None that he cared to share with you, at least."

"That was ten years ago, Laura. People change."

"Yeah, right, like leopards change their spots. You're out of your mind. You need to get straight, Kayla. I'm not going to watch you waste away. Not again. Not like you did when he broke up with you."

Kayla brushed past her sister. And though Laura had a point, there was something different about Allen this time around. Sure he had matured over the years, who hadn't? But this time, when they were together, there was a calm about him, a sense of belonging. And when they made love, he did so with all his heart and soul.

"Laura, you're wrong," Kayla replied then hopped back into bed. She didn't want to think about ten years ago, a time without Allen. All she wanted was to be left alone with her thoughts of him. She pulled the covers over her head.

"I hope so." Laura followed, then snatched back the covers. "For the sake of yourself, I hope you know what you are doing."

"I think I do. And if not, then I believe I'm old enough to handle it. Don't you agree?" She was more sarcastic than she meant to be, but to her, Laura had stepped out of bounds. Had been doing so for quite some time. "Besides, Laura, I think its time you let it go."

Laura sat on the edge of the bed. "I just don't want to see you hurt. That's all."

"Look, Laura I don't want to discuss this with you. Let's change the subject. Why are you here?"

"You didn't answer your phone. I thought something was wrong."

"The ringer must be off." She reached over and turned the ringer back on. Following her acceptance of Allen's proposal, they had returned to her loft and lain in each other's arms until the sun rose. She had turned it off, for she didn't want anyone or anything interrupting them.

"So, are you going to see him again?"

"Laura, what's it to you if I do?"

The look on her sister's face told all she wanted to know. She could see that Laura was not pleased with the attitude she was taking, but Kayla was finished with Laura's controlling ways. True, she was grateful to have a sister like Laura — she had always been in her corner, was always there for her, yet it was time to assert herself, handle her own affairs in her own way without her sister's interference. When she thought about it, Kayla was actually tired of her domineering ways. For as long as she cared to remember, Laura had been that way ever since their mother left them.

"You're being flip Kayla and I don't like it! You've changed. Allen has changed you!"

Kayla sat up. "No Laura! For once I'm going to handle things without your interference. This includes Allen. As a matter of fact, had you not interfered with Allen, I might have gotten the answers to my questions a lot sooner."

"What do you mean?"

She could see Laura was surprised. "Why would you threaten his life and then prove you meant it by showing up at his doorstep wielding a baseball bat? That was crazy and you know it. Had you just left well enough alone, he and I might have gotten past this — been able to go on with our lives without this cloud of uncertainty that has hung over us for what seems like forever. I don't blame him for not calling." She stood and faced her sister. "For ten years I've wondered why. Why he left me and why he never called. Well, I got my answers, Laura."

"Okay, you got answers. So what? That doesn't mean you have to continue going out with him."

"And why not? You seem to have all the answers today. All the right ways to do things. So, you tell me, why not see Allen again?"

"Get a grip, Kayla! Forget it. I'm through with it." Laura left the bedroom. Kayla followed her.

"No, Laura, I want to know. Tell me!" she grabbed her by the arm.

Laura reeled around and pushed Kayla, her back landing against the wall with a loud thud.

Kayla was stunned. In all their years, Laura had never laid a hand on her. Anger mixed with hurt rose up in her chest. Laura continued toward the door.

Kayla watched her sister casually pick up her purse and keys. She couldn't believe that her one and only sister had pushed her. Oh no, she thought, no one was going to lay a hand on her and get away with it. She had been raised by one person, Joseph, and not Laura! Kayla rushed up behind Laura and tackled her to the floor. They tussled with Kayla putting Laura in a half–nelson hold.

"What has gotten into you?" Kayla demanded. She tightened her grip. "I'm not letting you go until you explain this." Laura scratched at her hands, which only made Kayla more determined. "Tell me, Laura! What's gotten into you?!"

"When were you going to tell me Mom was back?" Laura blurted out, then began to sob. Kayla freed her. They both moved slowly, rising to sit near the door with their backs against the wall.

"How did you find out?" Kayla asked, then spied two suitcases sitting near the door.

"I walked into the house and they were just sitting there, laughing and talking like nothing ever happened," Laura began between sobs. "At first I thought I was seeing things. But when she stood and came toward me, I knew it was no joke."

Kayla helped her sister to her feet and led her to the couch.

"Oh, Laura. I thought Dad told you." Kayla said. "I'm so sorry you had to find out like that."

"What does she want, Kayla? I mean, after twenty years of nothing — no contact, no how-the-hell are you, she just pops up? This is too unbelievable."

Kayla squeezed Laura's hand tighter than she meant to. "I can't handle this, Kayla. I just can't."

"Did you talk to her?"

"Yup." Laura sniffed. "I asked her why she was back."

"Oh, no."

"Yeah. You know what she said?" Laura faced her sister. "Gave me some trite crap about missing us. That it was time for her to come home." She chuckled mechanically. "Home? Ah, what home? She gave that up a long time ago. Then she really tripped me out. Girl, she tried to hug me."

Kayla shook her head. "What did you do?"

"I slapped her hand away," Laura blinked, then looked at Kayla, a smirk stretched across her face. The pair burst into laughter, tears streaming down their faces. As their laughter subsided, both rubbed their faces with the backs of their hands. The slight motion made them double over into laughter again. It was a silent signal they shared whenever they were in trouble with their father, given just before they scurried in separate directions.

"I'm never going back there again." She sniffed. "What's going on, Kayla?" Why now? Why'd she come back now?"

Kayla was surprised. Laura had never asked her opinion — had never seemed to need anyone's counsel. It was always the opposite — Kayla searching and needing Laura's advice. She didn't like the pain she was seeing in her sister's expressive, pearl brown eyes.

"I don't know, Laura. I don't know. But you can stay here with me, you know that?"

"I'm sorry I pushed you, baby girl," Laura said using the nickname their father had given Kayla. "I was just so wound up."

"Why didn't you call . . . never mind, the ringer was off. Sorry about that. I didn't want anyone to wake me."

"I have a confession to make, Kayla." Laura looked down at her hands. "I've always liked Allen for you. I used to wish that he would just come around and make it up to you. Ignore me and my spiteful ways. You wouldn't have wasted

your time with Jonathan, or any of those other countless los-
ers, had I just left well enough alone."

"True that, but that isn't important right now. You are."

"Thanks, Kayla."

"That's what sisters are for. Take your stuff into the other
room."

Laura stopped her. She hugged Kayla tightly. "I really
appreciate this. I need some time to regroup. Try to sort
through all of this."

"Not a problem. You know I love you."

"And I love you, too."

Too much was happening too fast. Kayla didn't want to
believe that Jeanette was back. All of this was just not real.
Anger rose hard and fast, as she dressed quickly and left. On
the drive to her father's house, she thought of the lost little
girl she had been when Jeanette had abandoned them. And
for what? To chase some man half way around the world?
Jeanette had hurt them — had left indelible prints of pain
that always simmered just beneath the surface. Now that
pain, mixed with seething anger, rose and was about to bub-
ble over. But this time, the one who caused the pain would
experience just what it felt like.

Chapter 18

Kayla walked into her father's house, a beige brick three-bedroom Bungalow on the Southside of Chicago. Growing up, she had never lived anywhere else — they had never moved — and the inside was just as she had left it years before. And though Laura continued to live there, their father refused to change a thing. A few additional figurines that he had collected on his travels around the world and a large fifty-two inch color television set she and Laura bought him one Christmas were the only new items in the house. Everything else was the same — even the furniture. A cloth pale beige sofa, two wing-backed chairs in forest green, an oak oval coffee table, and two matching end tables — Queen Anne style, were still fastidiously arranged.

Her father hugged her as she stepped in. "Hey, baby girl, how's it going?"

"Okay, Dad. How are you?"

"I'm doing well, except for a little Arthur. I guess I'm doing okay for an old man."

She smiled at her father's unending joke about his arthritis. That seemed to be his only complaint — he wasn't a complaining man. She watched him walk toward the kitchen, marveling at how well he was aging. His warm brown skin belied his seventy years, and the mingling gray at his temples and throughout his still full head of curly hair, only added to his warmth. Kayla sat at the kitchen table.

"Where's Jeanette?"

Joseph kept his back to her. "Your mother went out with some friends. She'll be back in a little while." His words were so calm, as if Jeanette had never left. "Want some tea?" Joseph changed the subject.

Her eyebrows went up.

She watched her father's back as he went about setting a tea kettle on the stove, followed by his gathering cups and other various items for tea.

"Daddy?" she began. "Why didn't you tell Laura?"

He faced her. "I thought Laura was out for the weekend."

She turned up her nose. That wasn't what she wanted to hear. She wanted to know why he allowed Jeanette to come back, allowed her to insinuate herself into their lives after all this time.

Decades ago, her mother had walked out on them, left them so she could chase rainbows with some man who promised her the world. It had been devastating for them all. When she left, all she could say to them was that she had to follow her heart and for them to always do the same.

For months thereafter, Kayla and Laura had checked the mail and continually looked out the window. Every car, every letter, they had hoped was their mother telling them she was on her way home and that all would be okay. And whenever the phone rang, both had said a silent prayer, as they ran to answer it, hoping that it was her telling them to come and pick her up from the airport. But the calls never came. The letters never showed. And the cars held other people, not their mother. After a while, Kayla, Laura and their father stopped hoping and the three of them settled into routines. Joseph went about caring for them, and they went on about their lives, with Laura, being the oldest at fifteen, becoming the mother of the house. For every little thing, from a broken heart to a scraped knee, Laura played the role of mother. Yeah, she was grateful for Laura, but still she had missed her mother.

"Dad," she stood and touched his shoulder forcing him to face her. "When did she get back?"

"About a week ago."

"A week ago?! My, Lord!"

"I know." His body moved slowly, almost as if he were in pain. He sat in the chair across from her. "I thought I had time. Laura was in and out, staying with Brian and out of town for her job. I figured I would catch her before she came home. She surprised me. Surprised us both."

"Dad, Laura is a wreck. She's at my place now." Kayla looked into her father's deep brown eyes. A ring of grey circled the iris. "Where's Jeanette going to stay?"

"Here," she heard her father mumble. Kayla couldn't believe what she was hearing. This was just all too much for her to absorb. She sat down hard on the chair and stared out into space. "When did you say she'll be back?"

"In about an hour."

Kayla walked out of the kitchen and headed to her old room. The bright pink walls were just as she had left them, covered with various posters of artists and pictures of herself and high school friends. She eyed the posters of popular singing groups from the eighties and city festival bills — all plastered along the wall, telling of her life when she was younger, when things were easier. Simpler. She ran her hand across the old poster from the Taste of Chicago, the annual summer festival, where its once white background had turned a meek beige. She smiled weakly, reflecting on the memories of attending that year's festival. It was where she had met Allen.

She shook her head. Jeanette. It had been a long time, and a lot of miles, and a lot of unresolved feelings, she spoke to herself. Too much was happening all at once. Why now, she wondered.

She lay on the bed and closed her eyes. She didn't want to wait until her mother returned. As a matter of fact, she couldn't. Kayla wasn't ready to face her mother, even though curiosity gnawed at her, picking at her until she became restless. She rose, left her old room, then headed for the front door. She paused to look back at her father sitting on the couch. His eyes avoided hers. She shook her head as she closed the door behind her.

Kayla walked into the classroom. She was late for the final and she could see that her students were surprised. Not once during the whole semester had she been late for class. The past two weeks had been pure hell on her.

Laura had completely shut herself down. She had refused to speak to anyone but Kayla, and when she spoke, she did so in a monotone so low Kayla had to strain to hear her. And she wouldn't get out of bed. Several times their father came by, and tried to talk to Laura, but each time she just glared at him.

Kayla hadn't seen much of Allen, and though he had called often, she wasn't able to talk long. Jeanette's return had thrown the whole family into a dark labyrinth of uncertainty and anger. Even to the point of Kayla not being able to face her mother after all.

"Professor Martin, you're late," one student chided.

"I know, it's been a wild week," She replied, then scanned the faces of her students and was surprised to see Allen sitting in the rear of the class.

Dressed casually in a pair of jeans and a matching shirt, Allen watched her, a slight smile spread across his face. Kayla smiled back. She was truly glad to see him sitting there.

As Kayla began to give the instructions for the exam, she stumbled over her words, each syllable catching in her throat before flowing out. She coughed, attempted to clear her throat, but the words came out staggered and unclear. This had never happened before. She knew that the intensity of Allen's eyes, the way they followed her as she moved across the room, caused her to completely lose her train of thought.

Flustered, Kayla spat out the last of her instructions and sat down behind the desk situated at the front of the class. For the next hour, she stole furtive glances at Allen. When all but two of the fifteen students had finished the exam, Allen stood and moved to the front of the classroom.

"I want to know if everything's okay, Kayla? I mean, I know Laura's staying with you and all, but we haven't spent much time together lately?" He bent over and whispered in her ear, the warmth of his breath caressed the side of her neck.

"I know, baby. There's just so much going on. Laura's in a real funk and Dad's not too good himself. He feels he let us both down by allowing Jeanette to stay with him." She whispered back.

Kayla could see his face soften. "Is Laura going to be okay?"

"I hope so. I'm going home after this is over and check on her. If she's okay, maybe we can get together later."

"That's fine. I'm gonna go back to my seat now." He winked and returned to the rear of the class.

When the last student left, Allen rose. She watched him as he slowly stepped forward, his gait confident. She noticed the snug fit of his jeans. "You are really something else." He took her hand in his. "I am so proud of you." He kissed her hand. "You want to talk about Laura?"

Kayla nodded. "Yeah, I need to unload all of this madness on someone, but we'll have to walk and talk. I have to go see about Dad. But I have to go to my place first. I've got to get my car."

"That's okay, let me take you. It'll be good to see Joseph again."

She hesitated. "Ummm, I'm not sure about that."

Allen paused, then sat on the edge of the desk. "Joseph doesn't know we're seeing each other?"

"Well, actually no." She began to gather her things. She avoided his stare. It was only because of a chance run-in with Amina that Laura even knew she had been seeing Allen.

"I didn't know we were a secret," he stated flatly.

"We're not. It's just that . . . " she broke. How could she explain this to him. Her father, like Laura, had witnessed the results of their break up — had watched the unmistakable pain in her eyes. How could she tell her father that she was seeing him again, in love with him again? More so, how could she tell either of them that Allen had proposed and she had accepted. At that moment, Allen looked at her ring finger.

"Kayla, where's your ring?"

She averted his stare. "I took it off when I was washing dishes. I must have left it."

"Yeah right. What is it Kayla? Are you ashamed of me? You don't want anyone to know that we're giving it a second chance? Want to save face with your family?!"

His words had more bite in them than she wanted to hear. She hadn't even told Amina about the engagement. "Allen, its not like that," she lied.

He looked at her, his face a mask so solid, Kayla couldn't discern anger from pain. "Let's go." He ordered, then picked up her briefcase before he stepped to the door.

He was silent. The feel of his hand in hers was awkward, his motions stunted. Then she felt his hand surround her waist as he guided her from the elevator, through the outer doors and out onto the street. He switched places, moving her to the inside, closest to the buildings. His hand never left her waist.

"You want to tell me about what's going on with Laura?"

As they headed to Allen's car, she sighed and began to recount what she knew about the situation. The mere thought of her sister lying in bed, unbathed, hair tousled all over her head, made her uneasy. She knew Laura was hurt by Jeanette's departure and consequent return, and she had refused to talk about either situation. But through it all, Kayla had always held one image of her big sister, and her current state of depression wasn't it. Change was hard, she admitted to herself, but this was one of life's changes that Laura just didn't want to accept. Kayla then thought about herself after she and Allen broke up. She was just like Laura, only worse. All she had thought of, day and night, was the coldness in his words as he told her she wasn't the one he wanted to be with. How he had abandoned her, just like Jeanette had. Kayla looked at Allen's profile, the set square of his jaw. Fear rose fast and deep. The niggling voice was back and strong as ever. What if Allen abandoned her? His voice brought her back to the present.

"Why haven't you told your family about our engagement?" He pulled over and shut off the engine. "And I want the truth, Kayla."

"I . . I . .," she stammered. "Oh, Allen, its just that there's so much going on."

"You've already used that excuse," he replied snidely. "Now, you want to try a better one?" His eyes narrowed. "How about, you are afraid? Or do you think I'll leave you again?"

She evaded his stare. It was true. Not only didn't she want her family to dredge up the past, but she didn't want him to leave her again.

Kayla jumped at the sound of his palm hitting the steering wheel. "I can't believe you!" He yelled. "After all I've shown you. Went through."

"Went through?" Kayla found her voice.

"Yes. I enlisted Amina and Tim's assistance," he began. "They told me when you were free. If you were dating or not. And I needed to know, because I wanted you in my life, Kayla. I wanted the opportunity to prove to you that I'm not the same scared boy you once knew." He looked her squarely in the eyes. "I love you Kayla, always have and I always will. There's nothing you can do to change that." He turned away. "But what's the use. You're afraid. Afraid of what your family will say. And afraid to love. But things aren't always what they seem, Kayla. And things and people change. And I thought you had changed. "

The pain in his eyes was unmistakable. Kayla knew she had hit him low, had unwittingly pushed him away.

Allen started the car. He drove in silence, heading to her loft. He didn't look at her until he pulled up in front of her building. He remained silent. Kayla touched his arm. He flinched.

"Allen," she started, then changed her mind. There was no way to make him see, understand that she was afraid of tomorrow. True, she had told herself that this time things were different, but she had also hidden the fact that they were back together from her family. The truth of the matter was that she was embarrassed, felt weak for letting him back in her life after what had transpired years ago. She knew it would take a level of vulnerability she didn't own to explain it to him. Instead, she just shrugged her shoulders, then opened the car door. His voice stopped her.

"Kayla, all I ever wanted was to love you. And for the record. I wouldn't abandon you. I'd never leave you. Never." He turned his head.

Kayla closed the door and watched as he sped away, his tires squealing. The voice quieted. She wondered, what she had done. What had she done?

Chapter 19

"Daddy, why hasn't Ms. Martin been around?" Daniel asked as Allen stepped into their backyard. "I didn't mean to be rude."

Allen grabbed the football his son was tossing through an old tire which hung from the large maple in the middle of the yard, then faked a swish move just before tackling his son onto the grass. "Daniel, its not your fault. She's been having to tend to her family." He looked into his son's trusting eyes and remembered his promise to never lie to him. "Son, she may not be coming back."

"I knew it, Daddy, I knew it. She didn't want some ready-made family anyway."

"Who told you that?" Allen stopped.

"The woman at the playground."

"What woman?"

"Umm, I don't know. She was standing near the monkey bars the other day when me and Aunt Yolanda were there. I never saw her before."

"Where was Yolanda?" Allen tried to keep the panic out of his voice.

"At the ice cream truck."

"I see. Where's your aunt?"

"Did I do something wrong? I seem to be doing a lot of wrong lately." Daniel looked into his father's eyes.

"No, son, you haven't done a thing," Allen sat up and pulled Daniel into his arms. "Remember we started to talk about why Sharon and Keisha don't come around any more, well we will have that discussion after dinner. But right now I want you to remember what I said about talking to strangers. Okay?"

"Okay. No more talking to strangers. But dad, she said she knew you."

Allen froze. A fear rose in his chest and threatened to cut off his life, his very existence. He looked at Daniel, the warmth in his face. This was all he had in the world, the one thing that made his sun rise and set each and every day. God, how he loved this boy.

"Daniel, it's getting late. Time to go inside."

"Aww Dad, its still light out here."

"Barely, Little Man. Don't argue. Go inside, wash your hands and get ready for dinner."

"What's up?" Yolanda asked as Allen entered the kitchen.

"Did you see a strange woman talking to Daniel at the park?"

"What strange woman?"

"Daniel said some strange woman, who claims to know me, was talking to him while you were at the ice cream truck!"

"I was only gone a minute!" Yolanda said, her voice high with excitement.

Allen stepped to her. "Never do you leave my son for one second! Do you hear me?!"

Allen didn't wait for a response. He grabbed the mail from the counter, then mounted the stairs to his room. He thought about Kayla. He had lost her again, through no fault of his own, but he wasn't about to stand idly by and lose Daniel too.

Doubt surrounding his planned return into Kayla's life began to creep into him. The last thing he wanted to do was regret having re-entered her life. Maybe if he hadn't come on so strong, given her more space, more time; he began to second guess himself. Yet, time was the one thing he didn't feel either of them had. He didn't want to waste a moment on the regrets of yesterday and the fear of tomorrow. Yolanda losing her husband had taught him about time. Allen thought of her late husband, David. From the moment Allen met him, David was always so full of life and passion. He had lived his life like it would end tomorrow, and had loved Yolanda as if tomorrow would never come. He secretly wished for the type of love his sister had with David. It was complete and unconditional.

Allen had been impressed with David from the first moment they met. It was that passion that showed him what life was truly about, and over time Allen had come to see him like a brother. It had been David, two days before the accident, who told Allen to make it right with Kayla. Back then he had been too proud, too afraid to reach out to her, but not now. Now, all he wanted to do was to try and erase the pain he had caused her and love her as he should have, so they could live the rest of their lives fully and passionately.

His mind raced back to Kayla. The situation with her mother's return and Laura's depression over it only seemed to add to her blazing fire of fear and abandonment. I'd never leave you of my own will, Allen whispered into the air, don't you know that?

He sat down heavily in the large chair and swung around. The message light on his answering machine blinked. He pressed the button.

"Allen, my main man, this is Tim. Call me." Allen smirked. He knew that message meant loan.

"This message is for Mr. Allen Dawson. We are calling with a one time offer to . . ." Allen deleted that one.

"Allen," the voice began. A cold chill ran up his arms. The timid, shaky voice was unmistakable. In all his wildest dreams, he couldn't have made this up. He wondered how this could be happening to him. And why now? "It's Donna. We need to talk. I'll call back later."

He placed his head in his hands. This is too unreal. We've moved on, why is she back all of a sudden? This is a nightmare, he said. He played the message again and again. It was no dream, Donna had called. He wondered if she was the strange woman Daniel met at the park.

Allen looked at the photo of him and Daniel on his desk. He studied it. They shared the same features, the same wide smile. This was the son she left him to raise alone. He thought of all the nights of bad colds, tears from nightmares and scratches, and school events. He was Daniel's father *and* mother.

His mind went into a tailspin. He imagined himself standing in front of a judge, fighting for the only thing that had been constant, had been solid in his life. His son was the one thing that had really given his life meaning — made it worth living. There was no way she was ever going to take Daniel from him.

"Over my dead body," he swore and headed to the shower.

Kayla walked into the house, the familiar perfume greeted her as she made her way to the kitchen. Jeanette was here. She looked up to see her mother step into the room. She couldn't believe her eyes. After years of no contact, here she was, plain as day, standing in the very kitchen she once cooked in, combed her and Laura's hair in, and taught them how to bake in. A wave of anger swept over her and she grabbed her mother by the arm, whisked her toward the living room and stopped at the front door.

"Whoa, don't handle me like that, baby," her mother said and released her arm.

"Just what in the hell are you doing here?"

"And since when do you use such language with your mother," Jeanette's eyes were large.

"First of all, I'm grown. But second, and most important," Kayla stepped close into her mother's face, their noses
an inch apart. "I don't have a mother. Now, I don't know
what little game you are playing, nor do I want to know. But
if you think you're just going to waltz in here after twenty
years, you are sadly mistaken, sister. So, I suggest you crawl
back under whatever rock you came from and leave us alone!"

"Kayla," Jeanette rubbed her arm. "I have no intentions
of upsetting anything. I just wanted to see you and Laura."

Kayla laughed. She couldn't believe her mother was acting like nothing had happened. Like everything was just
okay.

"You've got to be out of your mind!" Kayla said. "In town
and wanted to see how we're faring?" she repeated snidely.
"Yeah, and I'm a millionaire. Come on Jeanette, tell me why
you're really here? I bet this is going to be some story." Kayla
stepped back, sat on the sofa, then crossed her legs followed
by her arms over her chest. Her mother moved toward a
chair.

"Oh, no. You can stand," Kayla barked. "This tale ain't
gonna take long. Then you can go and get your bags and
leave once you're done."

"Kayla, you hate me that much?"

The words stung. She could never hate her mother —
she had wonderful memories of the times they spent together. But she was also angry. Angry at having to endure the
pain of wanting her and not being able to hold her, of wanting to lay all her news of boys and school and dances at her

feet, just to hear her sweet voice say it would be all right. And to hear her sing — oh, could her mother sing. Each night she would sing to them in her sweet soprano as they lay in their beds. Kayla had loved her mother's voice, especially when she sang Brahm's "Lullaby."

"You don't understand, Kayla. I tried to . . . ."

"Tried to what?"

Jeanette sighed heavily. "How do I tell you that I found what I was looking for? What had been missing in my life? Had lived my life and accomplished what I set out to do? But I never stopped loving or thinking of you and Laura."

"Sure you did," Kayla replied nastily. "Besides, we never heard of any of your accomplishments."

Jeanette sat down. Kayla stood. "I said you can stand."

"Kayla, I'm tired. Your father and I were up till the wee hours looking at old photographs of you and Laura. My, what beautiful women you've both turned into."

"Yeah, save me the trip down memory lane," Kayla replied, then headed to the door. "As a matter of fact, why don't you save the whole story for someone who gives a damn. And let me warn you. If you so much as cause another member of this family any more pain, you will deal with me. Got that? Any pain."

Kayla slammed the door behind her, got in her car, then headed home. Her head ached as she replayed the events of the day. Impossible, was the only word she could find that described the whole day. Impossible.

"Girl, where have you been?" Amina teased as Kayla sat at the table. She waited until the waiter took their order before she let Amina have it, beginning with Tim.

"So, how's the love life with Tim? Seeing as how the two of you have had much pillow talk." Kayla caught Amina's expression. "Allen told me how the two of you helped him. Why?"

"Girl," Amina sighed, her gaze met Kayla's. "I know that Allen loves you. Always has. In the years that I've known you, you have been walking around with this load." She patted Kayla's hand. "You've been in and out of relationships, giving no man your heart. But if you are to truly go forward, you had to have closure with Allen. I know I should have kept my mouth shut, minded my own business, but you're like a sister to me, and I knew that Allen was the one you loved."

"But Amina," Kayla began with exasperation. "I needed to do this alone."

"And where has it gotten you?" Amina tilted her head to the side. "I spoke to Tim today."

Kayla bowed her head.

"My sister, you really need to look at yourself and think about what Allen is offering you. Who cares what people think?" Amina leaned over the table and settled her eyes firmly on Kayla's. "How often do you get a second chance at true love, to make right something that had gone wrong? Not often Kayla. Not often. This world is made up of folks who wish they could turn back the hands of time and erase pain, make up for past hurts. Hell, all he was trying to do was to love you. And you live by loving, girl."

Kayla couldn't meet Amina's eyes. Her mind filled with images of the loving days and sensuous nights she had spent with Allen.

Amina's voice was soft. "I just didn't want to see you continue to carry the pains of the past. Sister, can you forgive me?"

As Kayla reached out to take Amina's hand, she was interrupted by a tap on her shoulder.

"So, you've come to your senses," Jonathan sneered. "Hello Amina."

"What are you doing here?" Kayla got up. She wanted to face Jonathan, wanted him to see the seriousness in her eyes.

"I came to talk to you. I need you Kayla. I want you. I want to show you that I can love you. Allen could never love you like I do." His eyes pleaded along with his outstretched arms.

Kayla motioned for him to sit. She followed suit. "It's no good Jonathan. I'm sorry." She continued to look at him. "I know what happened between us. Our getting married was all wrong."

"No, it wasn't!" His glare became dark. "Don't ever say that."

From the corner of her eye, Kayla watched Amina who had delicately placed her hand on the nearby fork. Kayla thought hard. There had to be some other way to deflect, stave off the ensuing rage that simmered beneath Jonathan's angry glare.

"Jonathan, I've been less than honest with you," she held his gaze. "I knew back then, that we shouldn't have gotten married. You were in love with Serena and I was in love with Allen. We came to each other out of need, not out of love."

She watched as her words seemed to sink. And at the same time she began to feel free. Free from the lies that had been their only soothing comfort. She continued. "We both know this, Jonathan. We both knew that we were rebounding. We just didn't want to admit it. To ourselves nor to each other. And we owed each other that and didn't give it. I'm truly sorry, Jonathan, but we have to move on. We have to move on."

Jonathan shook his head. "I can't, Kayla. I can't forget how you felt in my arms. You made me forget. You made me feel like somebody. Things that . . ." He stopped abruptly.

Kayla twisted around in her seat and faced Jonathan squarely. "Serena, Jonathan. You mean Serena. You can't make her be what you want. You have to accept her for who she is. But tell me, honestly, that you didn't, still don't, love Serena?" He cast his eyes onto the table. "Tell, me the truth, Jonathan."

"Okay," he whispered. "I love Serena. But she's not you!" He looked into her eyes. "She never showers me with the kind of attention that you did, Kayla. The kind I need. You know?"

"Yes, I do, but Jonathan, it's over between us. It has been since the day we met. We were just too selfish to recognize, to realize that we were only holding on to each other out of fear."

Jonathan stood suddenly. Kayla saw Amina finger the fork. "I've interrupted your life long enough. I guess I didn't want to face the truth. But let me put this one thing to you." He raked his hand over his thick curly hair. "Have you faced the truth?" He turned his back, and walked quietly out of the door of the restaurant.

"Girl, what was that?" Amina demanded.

"Too much to go into now. I need to go home. There has been way too much drama for the past two days for me to stand it any longer." Kayla arose, reached into her purse, pulled several bills from her wallet, and left the restaurant.

She thought of Jonathan's words and knew the answer. No. She hadn't faced the truth. Hadn't with her family, with Amina, but more importantly with herself.

Chapter 20

Kayla stepped off the elevator and walked slowly, almost hesitantly toward her door. Inside, she stood and listened to the silence. After seeing Jeanette, Kayla had talked Laura into spending time with her boyfriend, Brian. Not that she didn't want her around, but more out of her own need to spend some time alone with her thoughts.

She winced at the roaming notions that skipped in and out of her head. Her mother's return. Jonathan's unexpected appearance at the restaurant. And her fears of her family knowing she was in love with Allen. The sound of the phone momentarily snapped her out of her self-induced trance.

"Hello, Kayla Marie Martin," her father greeted her.

"Hi, daddy. What's up?" She sat down on the nearby chaise and braced herself. Joseph only called her by her full name when he was angry with her.

"Oh, not a whole lot. Your mother told me about yall's conversation the other day. I think you were a bit hard on her."

"Hard on *her?* Daddy, I should have kicked her out, but it's your house."

"Kayla, baby, I know her return has wreaked havoc on this entire family, but I need you to know that Jeanette is here to stay. And though I have no intentions of getting back together with her, she is and will always be your mother, whether you like it or not. You know, sometimes people do things that even they can't explain. I've always tried to reach understanding. Not acceptance, but understanding. It's my way of moving forward. Now its your turn."

"Daddy, I can't. There is way too much pain."

"You forgave Allen, didn't you?"

Kayla figured Laura had told their father. "Well, yeah, I guess I did."

"Baby, I've made it a habit of protecting you and Laura. Keeping the truth from you both. But Jeanette's return made me see that it wasn't always for the best. So, now it's time you heard the whole story about me and your mother."

Kayla listened incredulously as her father went on to tell how he wasn't the husband her mother wanted or needed. He married Jeanette because she was pregnant with Laura, not because he was in love with her. When he discovered she had been having an affair, it devastated his ego, not his heart. He hadn't loved Jeanette and knew he never would, and his lack of love for her drove her into the arms of another man. He ended by saying that he was the one to put Jeanette out of the house, and subsequently out of their lives.

"I never knew, daddy."

"I know, baby girl, cause I never told you the truth. I just told this to Laura. You know that men can be odd creatures. Our hearts hurt much more easily and in protecting them we do crazy things. Much like Allen did ten years ago. He loved you, Kayla, but he was afraid of being hurt by your love. And as for Jonathan, I knew he didn't love you — knew it! And I regret not getting in the middle when you announced you were marrying him. We all knew you didn't love him, Kayla. We just sat by and let it all go down."

"Daddy, it's not your fault."

"I know, you're grown, were back then, but still had I explained all of this to you, you might have recognized that you and Jonathan didn't really love each other. And you wouldn't have made the mistake Jeanette and I did. And one other thing." She heard him breathe in deeply. "Can you forgive me for keeping your mother from you all these years?"

"Let me ask you a question?" Kayla began. "Why did you keep her from us?"

"Ego, baby, pure ego. I'm ashamed to say that I did it out of spite. I know it was wrong, but I couldn't help it. Now, I'm just sorry I did. Hell, look at Laura. She's got the outside strength of a Roman army, but inside she's frail. That's why she's always battling. Jeanette's return forced her to examine herself closely."

"Where's Jeanette?"

"She went to visit some friends. She'll be back tomorrow."

"Have her call me when she returns."

Kayla couldn't think straight. She was unable to answer her father's question of forgiveness. She hung up the phone then crawled into bed. Her head spun. She had no inkling that her father hadn't been in love with Jeanette; even worse, had kept Jeanette from them as a punishment for her seeking true love. It was so very ironic. Here they all were, going day to day searching for love from those who didn't have the capacity to return the love, while shutting out those who did. She thought of Jonathan and shook her head. She had been honest with him, hadn't sugar coated her feelings, but she hadn't been as forthright with Allen.

Kayla wanted Allen. Wanted to be with him morning, noon, and night. She wanted to love him without fear or hesitation. She knew it was time to face him; try and right her wrong. She only hoped it wasn't too late.

She picked up the phone and dialed his number. She listened to the familiar voice on the answering machine, left a message, then hung up. One down and one to go. Next was Jeanette. She had been mean to her, down-right cruel. Now that she had the truth, Kayla was ready to hear Jeanette's side of the story.

Allen sat at a table by the window at the small neighborhood bar and watched the clock. Donna had asked him to meet her at exactly 8:30 p.m. He looked at his watch. It was 8:20. In ten minutes she would be there, sitting across from him, asking for Daniel back — to be in his life. He was ready to do battle.

"Hi, Allen," he heard the voice behind him. He turned to see her standing at his side. "How have you been?" she asked.

"What do you want, Donna?" he looked her dead in the eye, startled by what he saw. She was a mere shell of her for-

mer self. Once extremely beautiful, Donna's smooth bronze
skin was marred by a puffiness and deep dark circles under
her eyes. Allen could have sworn she seemed lost, almost
distant as she returned his stare. He felt like she was some-
where else — in a world all her own. He looked away, down
to her hands. They were trembling.

"Well, that's a nice howdy do. No, nice to see you. No
how have you been? Jesus, Allen, its good to see you too."
She sat across from him. "I just want to see Daniel."

"Not possible," he stated evenly.

"What do you mean, not possible, Allen?"

"I do believe you understand the English language. I'm
not going to upset my son's life for anyone. Not even for you,
Donna. Especially not you!"

"Look, Allen. I just want to see him. That's all. Besides,
you might have a wife real soon, so I want to just lay eyes on
him before you let her be his mother."

"What the hell is that supposed to mean?"

"Nothing. It's just that you're probably dating, and you're
not getting any younger, so I figured you were looking for a
wife. And she's never gonna be Daniel's mother, you know
that, don't you? He has a mother."

"Had, Donna. Had!"

"I want to see him. When are you going to let me see my
boy?"

Allen looked deep into her eyes. The fear he felt when
Daniel talked about the strange woman returned. He felt

woozy, light headed as he began to connect the figure hiding in the shadows with her visit here. He stood suddenly.

"Let me warn you Donna," he began, getting right in her face. "You so much as come within one inch of Daniel! One inch! I'll kill you with my bare hands, so help me God. You got that?"

Allen tossed several bills on the table and began to walk away. The shrill in her voice stopped him cold. "I have rights, Allen. I'll take you and little Miss Kayla to court. Prove you are an unfit parent and she a detriment to my son's well being."

He twirled around. "Woman, you are out of your mind!" Allen grabbed Donna by her arms and lifted her from the seat. The patrons in the bar all looked their way, yet no one got up. "Seems as if you forgot one thing, Donna. You! You, walked out on us! So, don't expect any sympathy or well wishes. But make no mistake, come near me, Daniel, my house or Kayla, and you will regret the day you ever laid eyes on me. And you know me, Donna, I don't make idle threats."

He released her and headed to the door. Behind him he could hear Donna's voice — almost inaudible as she gasped for air — her incomprehensible spats.

It all made sense now, the odd feeling he had months ago, returned. It connected. Donna had been watching him all this time. Donna was the one Daniel saw at the park.

When her phone rang the next morning, she was hoping it was Allen.

"Hello?"

"Hi, Kayla," Jeanette said, her voice low and shaky. "Your father said for me to call you. Are you okay?"

How could she tell her mother that for twenty years she had yearned for her, wanted to be a part of her life, needed to feel her love up close, not across eons of water. Kayla had promised herself that she would be honest, lay her pain on the table, but she also now knew that everything wasn't as simple as she thought. Jeanette didn't walk out, she was forced out.

"Mother," she replied slowly. "We need to talk."

"I know. Let's meet for lunch, okay?"

Kayla agreed to lunch at BJ's Market on Stony Island. Her hands shook as she hung up the phone. Once showered and dressed, her last thought as she walked out the door was that of resolution. She had to come to terms with the fact that Jeanette was human and like herself, had sought love and found it.

The warmth of the June day shone on Kayla, as she stepped out of her car. A full summer-like breeze flowed around her sleeveless ankle-length tan, sage and cranberry print dress as she walked to the door of the restaurant. She wished the beautiful day would soothe her, make her sense of unsteadiness go away, but instead, she only felt confused from the chain of events over the past couple of days and the conversation she had with her father about her mother.

She spotted Jeanette sitting alone with her back to the door at a small table near the large picture window. Her shoulder length brown hair was pulled back into a pony tail and was held together with a hair clip of faux jewels. Her mother's warm features, much like her own, belied her true age.

Jeanette looked closer to forty than sixty. Her shape was not as supple as it once had been, but it still held its own. The only differences between Kayla and Jeanette were that Jeanette had honey-brown eyes — Laura inherited that — and an almost flat, wide nose. Kayla got her father's more rounded nose.

She walked slowly toward the table, images of the past flashing through her mind — her mother laughing as she pressed and curled her hair in the kitchen, evenings they sat on the porch and talked, nights when her mother stole into the room and tucked the covers about her. All the love she had buried for Jeanette now came to the surface in a flood of tears, and Kayla had to struggle to maintain her composure.

"Hi," she whispered, as she sat down, avoiding her mother's eyes. "How are you?"

"As well as can be expected," Jeanette replied. "This is a nice restaurant. Good choice."

For several more minutes the two exchanged meaningless words, and both seemed relieved to get up and go through the restaurant's line. Kayla settled on a bowl of gumbo and a corn bread muffin, while Jeanette chose to sample several of the soul food dishes.

When they returned to their table, Kayla could only think of the words her father had spoken: 'I made her leave.'

"There's so much to say and I'm not sure where I should begin."

"How about at the beginning. Daddy, told me why you left."

Jeanette sighed heavily, as the sparkle in her honey-brown eyes began to dull.

"I was in love with your daddy from day one," Jeanette began. "And I loved him like no other, haven't loved anyone since like that, but your father didn't share that — didn't feel the same. He did the honorable thing, as was customary in those days, and married me. We went to a justice of the peace in Cairo, Illinois, and I just knew I could make him love me. I set out to change him. And we both know you can only change yourself." Jeanette closed her eyes and winced. "After you were born, I went to Joseph and asked. . . . No, begged him to love me. That was insane and I knew it, but after nearly five years I thought he would grow to love me, you know?"

Kayla nodded and thought of her and Allen the first time around. Had she too tried to make him feel, be something he wasn't?

Jeanette continued. "Then about four years after you were born, I started going out. I had never been in a club, much less anywhere else. I was raised in the church, and church girls cooked, cleaned and cared for their families and went to church damn near every day. Church girls weren't supposed to have needs or wants. Anyway, I went to the famous Checker Board lounge. Had my first drink. And then

I saw him, Jackson. He was the bass player in this quartet. After their first set, he came and sat with me. We talked and talked, and after the show, I knew there was no turning back."

"What did daddy say?"

"What could he say?" Jeanette looked dead at Kayla. "He was rarely home. And when he was, he ate and went to bed. I felt as if your father was punishing me for loving him. I tried to be quiet and just accept what your father gave, but Jack had awakened in me a passion I didn't know I had."

"Okay, mom, I understand that. But why let daddy force you out? Why didn't you fight for us? We thought you loved us. Do you know how hard it was?"

"I tried, baby, I tried," Jeanette said, her voice rising. Patrons sitting nearby looked at them. "When he found out that I was going to divorce him, he told me fine, but the girls stay. I have never begged like I did that day. I was outside of my mother's house on my hands and knees. Now, don't get me wrong, Joseph was a good man, he brought home his check, took good care of us, and as far as I knew, never ran around. He just didn't love me, that's all."

"So you left?"

"It wasn't that easy. For nearly six months, every day, I called and begged Joseph to let me see you and Laura. He either flat out refused, or pretended y'all were busy. When Jack got a gig in Paris, he wanted me to go with him. Even when we arrived in Paris, I tried, but Joseph was so adamant.

I married Jack in Paris. And girl, tongues wagged, but I didn't care. I loved Jack."

Kayla sat back, her food untouched. She loved her father, loved the ground he walked on, but the reality of it all made him human, fallible. She didn't know what to think. And she sure didn't enjoy the thought of her father purposefully keeping Jeanette from them, no matter what. He hadn't loved her; why couldn't she be with someone who would?

"I sent you guys presents as Jack and I traveled around the world. And he loved me, Kayla," Jeanette whispered, tears forming in the corners of her eyes. "And I loved him back. Every emotion, every sensation I gave to him were the very ones I tried to give to Joseph. But I was young when I married your father, and I didn't understand what true love was until I met Jack."

"Where is Jack?"

"He died six months ago of prostate cancer. I brought his body back stateside, went back to Paris, where we had been living, packed all of our belongings and moved back here."

Jeanette let out a long sigh. "So, Kayla, that's the whole story. It's not that I didn't want you and Laura. It was that I couldn't have you. But I want us to start over. Do you think we can?"

Finally, like with Allen, she had her answers. In all her years, she had wanted her mother back, had wanted to lay her head in her lap and have her make the bad things better. But that hadn't happened, and she had learned to depend on

Laura and their father. Now here her mother was verifying the story her father had told.

"We can try. It's been so hard." Kayla replied, tears forming in her eyes. But now at least she had an answer. Finally she had the closure she had searched for her entire adult life. They embraced briefly, Jeanette whispering into her ear, "Baby, I'm so sorry. I really am."

Jeanette took Kayla's hand in hers. "From the bottom of my heart." Jeanette pulled a wallet from her purse. "Look at this." She fingered around the sides and found a piece of paper. "You made this for me when you were in sixth grade. It's the last thing you made for me." She held up the faded red cut out, the black words long since turned to gray, spelled out "I love you mom. Signed, Your Baby Girl."

Kayla took the heart. She remembered it. She also remembered what she had done afterwards.

"Mom," she hesitated. "After I made that for you, you left. And after a year of no contact I told all my friends you were dead." Kayla heard her mother gasp. "I know it sounds cruel, but it was the only way to get over you."

Jeanette reached toward her daughter again. "I understand."

No more words were spoken. For the first time since her mother's arrival, Kayla saw her in a different way. She no longer wanted to make her pay for the past; all she wanted now was for her to be here for the future.

"This has been some lunch," Kayla laughed through her tears, then looked at her mother's warm brown face. It's funny, she thought, what you think and what you know can certainly be two different things. Two entirely different things.

Chapter 21

Kayla ran to the phone. She looked down at the caller ID. It read pay phone. The number looked familiar. She picked it up.

"Bitch, I'm gonna get you. It's just a matter of time." The voice warned, then the line went dead. Kayla sat down on the sofa. Of all the calls before, none had been like this one. She placed her purse and keys on the coffee table, kicked off her sandals and headed to her bedroom.

She checked her answering machine. No one had called. She was disappointed that Allen hadn't returned her call. She looked around her bedroom. It was in complete disarray. To ease her mind, she began straightening — hanging up clothes and placing discarded shoes in their respective boxes, but she couldn't forget the angry, obscene call. Who would want to harm her? Kayla ran through a mental list, adding then deleting names. She could think of no one.

Kayla jumped at the sound of the knock on her door. Then spying the fireplace poker, she picked it up, and walked quietly toward the door. The knock came again. She peered out of the peep hole.

"Allen! How did you get up here?"

"I walked in. The lock was broken. You need to speak to the management company about that."

"I will," she replied. "Did you get my message?" She was glad to see him, but disappointed that he avoided her eyes. She could hardly blame him, in light of her childish antics. "Are you okay?" Allen remained silent. Instead, he stepped past her and sat down on the love seat. He looked up slowly. She saw fear in his face, in the deepness of his eyes. She too became afraid. The last time she saw fear in his eyes had been the day they broke up ten years ago. But this fear was different, more intense. She wanted to reach out to him, touch him, find solace for him.

"Allen, you okay?" Kayla asked again, her voice rose with the question.

"No, Kayla I'm not."

Kayla sat next to him and listened as he told her about Donna's call and their subsequent meeting. He ended by telling her he was afraid for them all.

"That may explain these hang ups." Kayla stood. She had never felt threatened before, had never felt a reason to be. With Allen's ex-wife back, the repeated hangups, then the threatening phone call, things did indeed seem too shaky.

"I want you to come and stay with me and Daniel until I can get a restraining order. I'll feel better if you do."

"Allen, I can handle her," Kayla said.

"I didn't say you couldn't!" he barked. She saw the worry lines creased in his forehead. He was serious. It was no time to argue. "I just want you close until this blows over."

"What about Daniel?"

"All he knows is that some strange woman has been lurking around. He doesn't know it's his mother."

"Allen?" Kayla took his hand in hers. "When are you going to tell him?"

"Tonight," he sighed. "I have no choice. When you show up with your stuff, he'll want to know why. Besides, I promised never to lie to him."

"Is Yolanda with him now?"

"Yeah, and Tim." He stood and shoved his hands into the front pockets of his slacks. "Look, I don't mean to rush you, but can you gather enough stuff for at least a week? We can come back if you need more. And you can forward your calls to my place."

Kayla ran to her bedroom, grabbed some clothes, books, CD's and other personal items and threw them into a suitcase. She gathered Patton and her things, turned off her answering machine, forwarded the calls to her cell phone, and headed out with Allen.

"Kayla?"

She turned and looked at him.

"Thank you. You don't know what this means to me."

During that week, Kayla, Allen and Daniel occupied the same space. In the beginning, after his father told him the whole story about his mother and the reason for Kayla's extended visit, Daniel had shut down. For nearly three days, the boy didn't eat and barely slept. At night he had nightmares, always waking up screaming for Allen. He finally spoke the night Allen had to work late. Tim came over to look after Daniel and Kayla.

"Uncle Tim's asleep," Daniel appeared in the doorway of Allen's home office. "Can I sit in here with you?"

"Sure, Daniel. Come on in." Kayla sat up from her prone position on the couch. She noticed the fear and anxiety in his young eyes and winced. She wanted to kill Donna herself for causing Daniel's pain.

Daniel pulled an ottoman from the corner and set it near the desk. He watched Kayla, close, almost as if he were trying to see through her. Kayla watched him watch her. She didn't want the boy to dislike her, but just the same she wanted him to come around on his own time.

"What are you reading?" Daniel asked.

"Oh, its a new novel by Eric Jerome Dickey. It's called *Liar's Game.*"

Daniel bristled. "I can read, you know? It says it on the cover there." He pointed to the book, then crossed his arms over his small chest. Kayla stifled a laugh. Male bravado at such a young age.

"So you can. But those are easy words. How about big words?"

"I'm the best reader in my class," Daniel boasted.

Kayla teased. "Prove it."

Daniel rose to grab Kayla's book. "No, not this one. One of yours. Got one?"

"Yeah, I got plenty. Come on, I'll show you." He grabbed Kayla's hand and led her to his bedroom. Along the wall stood a large oak bookcase, filled from top to bottom with books. Kayla smiled at the extensive library.

"You have a lot of books here. You've read them all?"

She watched Daniel poke out his chest. "Almost all. Daddy said great thinkers are great readers."

"True. So, what are you going to read to me?"

"How about this one?" He pulled a Star Wars book from the shelf. "You know the new movie is out. Dad said we were going to go see it, but then . . . ," his voice trailed off.

"I know. I want to see it too." Kayla sat on the floor. "When this is all over, you want to go with me to see it?"

Daniel's eyes sparkled. "You for real?"

"Yup. I'm a woman of my word. If I say we're going, then we're going."

Daniel sat next to Kayla and began reading. He read page after page about Jedi Knights and the Dark Side. Kayla enjoyed hearing his slight voice, his accurate pronunciation of each word he read. They were still side by side when Allen arrived.

"Dad!" Daniel ran and jumped into his father's arms. "Kayla's gonna take me to see the new Star Wars movie!"

"Sounds like a plan, little man." Allen kissed him on the cheek. "Hey its time for bed. Get your pajamas on, and I'll come and tuck you in."

Daniel looked at Kayla and smiled. "Can Kayla come, too?"

Allen placed Daniel on the floor and looked at Kayla. "If she likes. Maybe she'll read both of us a bedtime story."

Daniel giggled. "You're too old for bedtime stories."

The three laughed, Daniel's voice could be heard as he left the room singing a made-up tune about going to the movies.

From that moment forward, she and Daniel spent hours reading to each other and seeking new adventures. She taught him how to play marbles and he taught her how to play PlayStation. And every evening, she prepared and ate dinner with Allen and Daniel, followed by, at Daniel's insistence, her reading to him each night before bed. Without a second thought, Kayla had become a part of their everyday existence, and she and Daniel grew closer and closer. When one week had turned to two, due to Allen's inability to get a speedy restraining order because Donna had disappeared, Daniel had asked her if she were going to stick around. It was at this point that she knew her life would be empty without Allen and Daniel.

On the day Kayla planned on going back to her loft, Tim had come and taken Daniel on an outing. Kayla knew it was now or never, and she was afraid. In the time she and Allen had been under the same roof, they hadn't mentioned one word about their relationship. Kayla felt she needed support. She called her father.

Joseph listened intently as she told him the whole story, including the real reason why she was staying at Allen's house. In the end, her father told her to follow her heart —

that he knew she loved Allen and wouldn't be happy unless
she allowed herself be in love with him.

When she hung up, Kayla sat motionless on the couch in
Allen's home office and tried to think of what she would say
to him. Her thoughts were interrupted when she heard him
climbing the stairs. He stood in the doorway.

"Thank you, Kayla."

"For what?"

"My little man has a few sparks in his eyes."

Kayla was relieved. "Was nothing. He just needed some
reassuring. That's all."

Allen moved to sit beside her. "And so do I, Kayla."

It was time. Time to face the threatening demons.

"So, what are we going to do?" he asked. "I like having
you around here, Kayla. Plus, Daniel asked me today if you
were you going to stay. Like forever. And his daddy wants to
know the same." He took her hand in his. "Kayla, you can't
run from this, and you know it."

Kayla was ready to lay her fears on the table, to finally be
vulnerable to him. She had made up her mind.

"Allen, let me apologize to you," Kayla rose from the
couch. His eyes bore into hers and she could tell he was
holding his breath, bracing himself for her to reject him a
second time. "I was wrong, baby. All wrong. I want to spend
the rest of my life making it up to you. You were right. I was
afraid of a lot of things." She sighed. "I have come to love
you more than I expected, Allen. And being here with you

and Daniel, caring for you both, I've come to realize that I don't want to live without either of you."

Allen straightened. "What are you saying, Kayla? You have to make it plain to me. I don't want to assume."

Kayla pulled him into her arms and looked into his eyes. "I'm saying," She took a deep breath. "I don't care about anything other than loving you. Allen Dawson, I will be your wife; that is, if you can forgive me. If you still want me?"

Allen stared at her. A hint of disbelief crossed his face. Kayla stroked the sides of his face, got on the tips of her toes, and kissed him. He held her close.

"Kayla, are you sure? I can forgive you, but I need for you to be sure about this. About us."

"I'm sure, Allen. I allowed yesterday to get in the way of our tomorrow. Now I'm crystal clear about what I want. And I want to fall asleep and wake up in your arms, each and every day of our lives."

"Oh, Kayla, you won't be sorry." He watched her as she stepped from his embrace, then pulled the engagement ring from her pocket. Allen took the ring from her, got down on one knee and took her hand in his. He placed the ring on her finger, kissed her hand, then rose. He pulled her into her arms, whispering. "I'll spend the rest of my life making sure you're never afraid."

Kayla nodded her head and kissed him. He returned her kiss, his tongue tracing sensuous circles around her lips. She had missed him, had missed his arms around her at night. She placed her hands upon his smooth face, then kissed his lips — her hands made an imaginary trail up and down his back. He moaned as she intensified the kiss; her tongue lingered long with his.

He eased onto the floor, taking her with him until she was parallel with his body. They moved against each other, their lips locked. His hands left hot embers at each spot, his moans seeped into the crevice of her soul. When she felt his hardness, she knew that there was no turning back. And in her heart, she didn't want to.

"You won't regret this, Kayla." He broke the kiss. "I promise you, you won't ever regret marrying me."

Kayla smiled. "And I don't expect to."

Allen gently slid Kayla from him. He stood and put his hand out to her and then lifted her up into his arms. "Kayla, I love you," he whispered, her head resting on his shoulder as he carried her to his bed.

He laid her down and began to undress her. He took off each piece of her clothing slowly, methodically pausing to let his eyes followed by his lips take in each exposed part of her. Once he had discarded her bra, followed by her panties, he looked at her. His eyes were different, more passionate than before. A wicked chill raced up her body.

She enjoyed watching him undress, the deliberate way he seemed to tease her with his fluid motions. He was never in a hurry, and Kayla thought that if she had at least twenty years of this, she would be eternally happy. As he stood in searing red jockey briefs, a favorite of hers, his waiting member strained against the fabric, she couldn't imagine him any more sensuous, or her wanting him any more than she did at that moment. His body called to hers and she put her arms out to him.

"Kayla," he began as he joined her on the bed. "This is where you belong. Here, in my life, in my heart and in my bed." He began to tease her breasts. "I don't ever want us to be apart. You hear me?"

All she could do was nod. His nibbles and kisses were beginning to affect her and she heard herself moan. He wouldn't let up. Instead, he sucked in her nipple, his tongue flicked across it while his free hand kneaded her other breast. He began to move, graciously placing wet kisses along her entire body. Again, making love to her from head to toe. Each movement caused the passion between them to intensify. And just when she felt she could endure no more, he turned her over on her stomach and kissed her up and down the full length of her body, stopping at her sumptuous behind, where he paused to leave wet evidence. She was beside herself. She had had enough. He had started them. Now she was going to finish.

Kayla stopped him, rolled him over and removed his briefs. She began to kiss him, beginning with his lips, down his chest, across his stomach and then to his member. She teased him. The more he moaned and begged, the more she teased, refusing to let up on her own skillful game of seduction.

He pulled her gently by her shoulders. She wriggled away and lay on the bed. She took his hand to her feminine being and guided him, moving his hands in short, deliberate circles. She closed her eyes, the surge eased its way to the top. Her hips began a sensuous dance. When she felt the surge become stronger, knew the release was near, she let it absorb her. She arched her back and cried out.

Kayla breathed heavily, beads of sweat appeared upon her face. When she opened her eyes, Allen was smiling at her. He started to say something, but she wouldn't let him, instead she placed a wet kiss on his lips and pulled him atop her. She wasn't finished with him. She would never be.

"Woman, you are driving me wild," he breathed huskily as he entered her.

He began to move, she moved with him. Their hips moved first against and then with one another. She placed her legs around his hips, pulling him closer, deeper. His languid movements matched hers. The more he moved the closer she came to yet another surge. She held him off. Kayla signaled for them to roll over. She wanted to really love him, the way she knew she could. She sat atop him — her fingers played in the smooth and silky hairs on his chest. She watched him as he closed his eyes and let her have her way. When she moved, tightening her grip on him, he reached out and pulled her to him, their lips met. He kissed her with a wanton fever and began to move his hips with hers. She placed her arms behind his neck and nestled her head on his broad chest, the soft hairs rested on her cheek. Kayla could tell he was close, ready to release inside of her. She circled her hips, her own strokes matched then exceeded his. His fingers became tangled in her hair — his free arm wrapped tightly about her waist. His moans turned to words of endearment as she attempted to bring him to his peak. His body tensed. She felt his member throb. He released her hair, held her with both hands and rolled her over. They began again.

Allen's motions were smooth and deliberate. He slowed his pace, watched her face as he did. When she attempted to move against him, he paused. He teased her for long moments until neither could keep the passion from erupting. Kayla put her arms around him, held him, then began to undulate beneath him. They were fluid — as one, as they moved toward the surge that begged to be released. His movements became more pronounced, as did hers. Her embrace tightened as she felt the surge move up her legs and across her whole body. She moaned loudly when she felt it, felt the surge then surrendered to it, to Allen. She cried out his name as she forced her hips into his.

Tears streamed out of her eyes as she held onto him. All the emotion — all the love she felt had surfaced. In an instant, Kayla knew they were never going to part. Something in her said so and it was what she had always wanted. To love and be loved. But more important, she wanted to be loved by Allen.

They held each other. Neither wanted to be the first to move. Each wanted this day — this feeling — this moment to last forever.

Chapter 22

Kayla felt like a school girl. After being holed up in Allen's house, she was glad to be out among people again. He had finally secured a restraining order against Donna. Following, Kayla reluctantly moved back to her loft. She didn't want her future stepson to think it was okay for a man and a woman who weren't married to live together as if they were. And though he didn't want her to leave, he seemed to understand when she explained her reasons to him.

At Amina's suggestion, she agreed to go on a double date with Amina and Tim.

"Girl," Amina sighed. "I really like that man."

"I see," Kayla smiled and adjusted her sunglasses. She watched in apt amusement as Allen and Tim attempted to win teddy bears at the shooting range. For Kayla, it had been decades since she had been to a street carnival. The smell of freshly popped buttered pop corn, the aroma of it wafting up into the air, called forth memories of being young again. Then there were the throngs of people — especially the teenagers, coupled and holding hands. She began to feel like a teenager herself.

Amina tapped the diamond engagement ring on Kayla's ring finger. "So, when were you going to tell me?"

"It just happened. I finally came to my senses. I called Dad and Laura the day I accepted his proposal. They are thrilled."

"And, what does that have to do with me? I'm your best friend."

Kayla put her arm around Amina's shoulder. "That you are. We're going to get married in August. The eighteenth to be exact. We've both been there before, so its going to be very small. Laura's going to be my maid of honor. And I want you to be a bride's maid."

"Sorry about my telling Laura." Amina sighed.

She laughed. "Girl, it's all good now. Laura is too happy for us. She said we belong together."

"I'm glad to hear that, because that expression in her eyes when I told her about you and Allen was deep."

"Laura's reaction had more to do with our mother's return than with my seeing Allen again."

"How's she doing now?"

"Coming around. She and Jeanette have been spending time together."

"And what about you, Kayla?" Amina looked her in the eye. "Have you come around?"

Kayla thought for a moment. "Yeah, I have. I can't believe all that has gone on. And I want to thank you for opening my eyes. I love ya, sis."

The pair embraced. "I love you too. Just be happy."

The two became silent. They turned their attention to Allen and Tim. Tim held a large white teddy bear in his arms and grinned as they approached. Allen held a large grey elephant.

"Okay, you shot that last duck," Allen huffed, then laughed. "He wanted to be shot."

"Hey Tim, did you know about this?" Amina pulled Kayla's hand upward. Tim raised his eyebrows.

"I take it that's an engagement ring."

"You take it right," Allen responded then took his brother's outstretched hand.

Kayla watched the two bothers. The familiar resemblance was uncanny, but the love they shared was unmistakable. She could see the happiness wash over Tim's bright brown eyes as he pulled his brother to him and gave him a hearty hug.

"'Bout time," Tim said, then laughed. He excused himself and Allen followed.

Tim stopped Allen at the stall. "I know you're a grown man, so I'm not going to lecture you like some kid. When we were young, I was so protective of you, wanted my baby brother to be and have the best. I have never been prouder of you and you've given me a great gift in Daniel." Tim eyed Allen. His eyes became misty. "Now, to Kayla. Lil' Bro, I have never seen her this happy, ever. And I know I've said some crazy, chauvinist things in my time, but she's the one, Allen. So, you need to make sure that smile on her face never fades and those lights in her eyes never dim."

Allen looked at his brother and hugged him again. "Thanks, Tim. I love that woman, and I'll spend my life making sure I never hurt her. I'll go to my grave loving her. Hey, what about you and Amina?"

"Umph," Tim grinned. "That woman does things to me, man. Makes me think about many tomorrows."

Allen smiled. In all his years, he had never heard Tim talk about anything other than fixing cars and surviving. He prayed that maybe, just maybe, his brother had finally found what he had been searching for his whole adult life for.

Both men exited the bathroom. Kayla watched them. Allen a fraction shorter than Tim, as they walked toward the bench she and Amina shared. Kayla stood, took Allen's hand in hers, and began to walk. Amina and Tim followed behind them. She looked up at Allen. He winked at her then squeezed her hand.

"Is every thing okay?" she asked.

"Couldn't be better, love."

With the month of June nearly gone, Kayla became enthralled in planning her and Allen's wedding. And though Allen had gotten the restraining order against Donna, she hadn't shown her face since the night she met Allen at the bar.

Things had returned to normal. The obscene phone calls stopped, and there was no sign or hint of drama. Everyone went about their normal routine. Jeanette had moved from her father's home and found herself an apartment overlooking Lake Michigan. And Laura was spending time with their mother. Finally, things were back to normal and everyone was ready to move forward.

Kayla stretched her long arms wide, then grinned at the thought of becoming Mrs. Allen Dawson. She had spent the entire day at the bridal shop with her mother, Laura and Amina picking out bridesmaid dresses and a dress for her mother. Kayla had only smiled at the expression on her mother's face as she modeled a pearl taffeta tea length dress adorned in iridescent beading, small enough to give off just a hint of its splendor in the light.

Amina and Laura had chosen a similar dress. Laura's was a deep peach, and Amina's was the same hue, but lighter. As for Kayla, she chose a floor length, off the shoulder cream colored floor length dress, with ornate beading at the bodice.

Following the dress selection, the group had lunch at Kayla's favorite restaurant, Dixie Kitchen and Bait Shop, in the Hyde Park community. There was much laughter as Jeanette told Amina stories of Kayla and Laura as little girls. Kayla had listened in utter fascination as if she were living them right then and there. Yeah, there were some events in their lives that Jeanette had missed, but having her back more than made up for it all.

Kayla took off her T-shirt and jeans, put on her plum-colored nightgown, and slid into bed. She thought of Allen and Daniel. To think, all of this wouldn't be happening had she not come to her senses and listened to her heart. She yawned then closed her eyes. Sleep came easily.

The sound of the jangling phone startled Kayla. She glanced at the digital clock on her night stand, anger stirring as she saw the dial read 3:30 a.m. She picked up the phone.

"Whoever this is better already be dead," Kayla answered groggily.

"Naw, Bitch. But you're going to be. You'll never make it down that aisle." Then the phone went silent.

Kayla sat straight up in bed. She looked around her, her eyes wide with fear. She slammed the phone on its receiver and thought this couldn't be happening again. The calls had stopped it seemed just around the time when Allen got a restraining order against his ex-wife. There was no way it was her.

She turned on the lamp and dialed Allen's number. She tried to steady her hands as she listened to the outgoing message of Allen's line. Then it hit her. Allen and Daniel were on a fishing trip and wouldn't be back until the day after tomorrow. She placed the phone on the cradle. Her mind raced, as she tried to think of who she should call next.

"Amina. Yeah, I'll call Amina. She'll come over and keep me company." She picked up the phone, dialed her number. She placed the phone back in its base when Amina's voice mail came on the line.

Kayla jumped out of bed, dressed quickly, grabbed her purse and headed toward the door. The only other place she would truly feel safe was with her father.

Chapter 23

"Mr. Martin, have you heard from Kayla?" Allen asked over the phone. "I called her several times and got no answer. Then when I got back today I called and even went by her place. Her neighbor said she hasn't seen her."

"No, I haven't and I was about to call you. We haven't heard from her since late yesterday when they went to the bridal shop. It's not like her to miss a day without calling."

Allen paced the floor of his office. He had an odd feeling he couldn't shake. He had called everywhere before calling Kayla's father. He even called the Chicago Police Department to make sure that the restraining order he had against Donna was still intact — he needed to be sure that she was far away. If Donna had harmed Kayla, he would see to it that she spent the rest of her natural life in a padded cell. He ended his calls by placing one to a private detective. The same one he had hired to search for Donna years ago.

"I'm on my way, Mr. Martin." Allen hung up, then feverishly dialed his home number. Upon speaking to his sister, Yolanda, and ensuring that she and Daniel were safe, he rushed out of his office.

Memories flooded Allen as he parked his car in front of the house Kayla grew up in. He recalled the lazy days he had spent sitting on the front porch with her, his hand in hers, as they gazed at the moon and talked about their futures. Allen felt a wave of regret wash over him. Too much time, he felt had been wasted living for what wasn't important, while letting what was important slip away. Not this time, his mind shouted, I won't let this happen.

"Allen, its good to see you again."

"Same here, Mr. Martin."

"No, call me Joseph."

Allen looked up as Jeanette walked into the living room. He had never met Kayla's mother, yet he could see that she had the same warm brown face as Kayla. He stretched out his hand. Jeanette pulled him into an embrace.

"Honey, that's too formal." She tightened her embrace. "Especially for folks about to become family. How are you doing?"

"I'll be better once I know where Kayla is."

"We all will," Jeanette responded, then sat next to Joseph.

He glanced over to his left and spotted his brother and Amina sitting close, their hands entwined. Tim stood and walked over to him.

"We're going to find her," Tim said, then pulled his brother into his arms.

"Yes, we are," he replied, then moved to kiss Amina on the cheek. He eyed Laura as she sat silently in a green wingback chair, her hands folded demurely over her lap. Allen resisted a snuff. He pictured her with that red bat. Her actions still stung. He was surprised when she rose to greet him with a kiss on the cheek, but the pain in her eyes betrayed her. He didn't know why, but Allen thought of the Judas. He shuddered.

"Allen, you're looking well," she remarked cooly. He nodded, then forced his attention to Joseph as Laura returned to her seat.

"I think we should call the police." Joseph interrupted. "It's been over twenty-four hours." Everyone nodded in agreement.

"Okay," Allen began. "I have a private detective looking for her as well."

Laura spoke up. "That's a good idea." She came to stand in front of Allen. "Dad, go ahead and call the police. Allen and I are going out to get some fresh air. We'll be right back." Laura pulled him gently by his arm.

Allen motioned for Laura to get in his car. She remained silent as he drove around several blocks then stopped across from a park. He watched as Laura's hand wrung one over the other. He stepped out of the car. They hadn't spoken in ten years. He looked at her. Her eyes were red. She looked away quickly.

"Let's walk," Laura said. Allen fell in step beside her.

"You know Allen, I have yet to apologize for my actions some years ago," she began. "Kayla is all I really have. I mean, dad did a great job taking care of us and all, and I love him dearly, but it was Kayla who gave me a reason to rise in the morning. Upon Jeanette's return, and yours, I realized that I was the one who needed her. Not the other way around."

He was stunned. He had never associated her and humility in the same vein, especially after the break up between him and Kayla.

"And for the record, Allen, I really like you. I like you for Kayla. Always did. Back then you seemed to complement the woman she was growing into, and now the woman she has grown into. She's not the little sister I want her to be. Even though I tried to keep her as such."

He watched as tears rolled down her cheeks.

"Allen, can you forgive me? Back then, when you and Kayla broke up, she was so devastated, so sad. The fire in her eyes had gone out completely and I was afraid she would never be the same, that she might not make it. And she had already suffered enough. We both had."

He took her hand in his, then pulled out a handkerchief, dabbing the corners of her eyes. "Laura, I don't hold it against you. I really don't. You were protecting Kayla, that's all. I just wish I hadn't hurt her."

"Me too."

"But all that is in the past, Laura. I love Kayla. I want her with me until I breathe my last breath. And that's heavy, I know. But all I can do now is to show her how much she means to me. As to forgiving you, that was done long ago. I understood, Laura. I may not have liked hearing what you said, but I did understand. Besides, I don't think we'd be together today had I not heeded your warning and stayed away."

"Thank you, Allen. Thank you for understanding."

He hugged her. "Not a problem. Now, we have to focus all of our energies on finding Kayla."

Suddenly his pager went off. He checked the display, jumped to his feet, and ran to his car. He pulled his cell phone from the middle console compartment, then began to feverishly dial the number from the display.

"When did this happen?!" Allen shouted into the phone. "Are the police there? I'm on my way!"

"Let him go! He's not your son! He'll never be your son!" Keisha shouted at Kayla as she pointed the gun in her direction. "Get over there and sit down!" Keisha's voice changed, became softer. "Come here, Daniel, baby, sit next to me."

Daniel shook his head slowly. His hand held onto Kayla's tightly. She looked down at Daniel, his dark eyes were just like Allen's. She winked at him, forced a smile, and motioned him to stand slightly behind her. If either was going to walk out intact, Kayla knew she had to gain control of the situation, think of some way to talk Keisha out of killing them.

"All I wanted was for Allen to love me, like he loves you," Keisha said as she peered out the window at the half dozen or so police squad cars dotted in front of Allen's house. "No, I wasn't good enough. I wasn't Kayla."

Kayla watched her mouth move, then her eyes. She looked for some waiver, some sign that Keisha was tired. For over twenty-four hours, she had held Kayla hostage, taking her at gun point when she walked out of her loft. When Keisha approached her and spoke, Kayla instantly knew she was the strange woman who appeared at her office.

Dressed in a white, fitted wedding gown, Keisha introduced herself as Allen's wife to be, then forced Kayla to drive to an old abandoned warehouse not far from her loft, where she continually dialed a number on her cell phone. Then without warning, she had Kayla drive to Allen's house and forced Yolanda out, demanding that she leave Daniel behind.

"I just knew you were gone for good when Donna showed up. I was there. I spotted that crazy chick immediately. She's really insane, you know that? And as crazy as she seemed, I just knew your ass would be dead. But no, you're here about to marry the man I'm supposed to be with. You think you're going to play mommy to the boy I'm supposed to be a mother to. No, sister, I don't think so. I've worked too hard."

"Keisha, come on girl, let me and Daniel go," Kayla said softly. "You and I both know he's not worth all of this." She pointed to the gun. "Do you want to spend the rest of your life in prison? If you kill us both, then Allen will never forgive you."

"Oh?" Keisha's eyes turned a deep black. "You didn't know? I'm not gonna lay a hand on Daniel. Not my sweet baby. No, I'm going to kill you. Then Allen, Daniel and I will live happily ever after. Amen!"

Kayla's eyes widened. Thoughts of her father roamed through her head, followed by images of Jeanette, Laura, and then Allen. She couldn't think straight. How did all this with Keisha begin? Allen had mentioned her once, talking about the way she reacted to their breakup.

"Your ex-husband, Jonathan, is some piece of work, you know that?"

"Oh? How do you know Jonathan?"

"He and I had a baby." Keisha laughed wickedly when she saw the shocked expression on Kayla's face. "You didn't know?" Kayla shook her head. "Yeah, he was so wrapped up into you and that other fool, what's her name?"

"Serena," Kayla answered softly.

"Yeah, that's it. That's her name." Keisha waved the gun. "But he didn't want us. He didn't want that beautiful baby girl. He wanted me to have an abortion, but I refused. Flatly refused. She was all that I had."

Kayla couldn't believe what she was hearing. She knew Jonathan had plenty of women, for every time she had seen him around the city he was with a different one, she didn't know he had dated the crazed woman standing in front of her.

She shook her head slowly. This was all too much. Some sick nightmare with no ending. Her body began to waiver. Lack of sleep compounded with no food or water taking its toll. Yet, she knew she had to remain standing, if not for herself, then for Daniel. She looked down at him, then up into Keisha's eyes. The deranged look was more intense, unsure. Up to this point, Kayla had watched her closely, trying to gauge her unstable emotions, which went from frightened to pure hate.

"Keisha, if you hurt me who's going to take care of the baby you had with Jonathan?"

Keisha shifted her weight and placed her left hand on her hip. "Your lying, snake of an ex-husband didn't tell you?" She waved the gun around. Her voice changed again, this time it was sweeter, almost childlike. "My precious Nakiah died."

Kayla raised her eyebrows, then inched forward. "Keisha, I'm so sorry," she whispered and held out her left hand toward her, while keeping her right one solidly on Daniel's chest. "I didn't know about that," she said. "How did she die?"

"She died in her sleep. That beautiful baby died in her sleep. She was the only thing worth anything to me. I was a good mother. I really was. I checked on her just about every hour, on the hour. She was sleeping peacefully, like she always did. She was such a good baby. Then all of a sudden she wasn't breathing. But, she was even more beautiful that day, as she lay there in her crib. And how she looked just like Jonathan, her curly hair." Her voice became harsh again. "That ass! That ass is why my Nakiah had to go."

Kayla stopped in her tracks. She tried to understand what Keisha was saying — tried to keep her words intact. She wasn't sure if she had heard her correctly.

"And Jonathan was never around. He just stopped calling after the baby was born. You want to know how I know about you and Allen?" Keisha smirked.

"Sure, why not."

"When I met Jonathan, all he talked about was you. How beautiful you are. How smart you are. How good you are. Kayla! Kayla! Kayla! It was all I ever heard. But he said you were in love with Allen and not him. He was in love with you. Did you know that?" Kayla shook her head in response. "Well, he was and I tried everything in my power to change his mind. But he couldn't seem to let you go. Then I met Allen about two years ago at his company's Christmas party. He was so nice, so attentive, but he too was caught up in you. I knew this when I found the letter from his ex-wife. At that point, I knew exactly why Allen wouldn't commit to me. You're a regular home wrecker, you know that?"

"No, I'm not. All I know . . . ."

"You don't know shit, Miss Thang! Tell me, what do you know?"

She wanted to change the subject from Allen, deflect her attention. If she could keep her talking about Jonathan, she might have a chance. "Well, I know all about Jonathan, that's for sure."

Keisha huffed. "Girl, why did you marry that fool? You didn't love him! Besides, he ain't all that. Hell, he ain't even good in bed. How did you put up with him for so long?"

"I don't know how I did it, Keisha, to be honest with you," Kayla replied and resumed moving toward her. "All I know is that you're absolutely correct about Jonathan. He ain't right." Kayla laughed slightly and inched forward again. "I mean, all the women and such."

Kayla was now less than five feet away when Allen suddenly appeared in the doorway. Keisha whirled around, the gun pointed at him. Kayla rushed up behind her, grabbed Keshia's hand holding the gun, and struggled with her. She could feel Keisha's strength, and she prayed to her creator to help her match or exceed the crazed woman's brawn.

Allen grabbed Keisha's hands and attempted to push Kayla away. She watched in horror as Keisha kicked Allen in his chest, the swift movement knocking him off balance, causing him to land on the floor. Then Keisha faced Kayla, and they continued to struggle, Keisha bringing the gun within inches of Kayla's chest. In an instant, Kayla overpowered her. They tussled, Kayla's hand firmly on Keisha's. Kayla shut her eyes as the shot rang out.

Chapter 24

The cars followed one behind the other, lights on, hazzards flashing, as the procession headed up the tree lined street. The sun shone brightly, its hot rays beaming on the people who stopped along the way to watch the white stretch limo snake around the corner before heading to the main artery as it led the procession to the Dan Ryan Expressway.

"Here's to forever," Allen kissed Kayla on the lips, then raised his champagne filled glass. Kayla smiled at him and thought of how they almost didn't make it to this glorious day.

When Allen had stepped in, he attempted to grab Keisha's hands. Daniel had screamed at the sound of the gun firing. Luckily, the bullet lodged into the wall behind them, with Kayla finally removing the weapon from Keisha's grip. Kayla was so angry, that Allen had to pull her from atop Keisha just as she began to slap the woman several times across her face.

"You have truly lost your mind!" Kayla had screamed as she kicked at Keisha lying on the living room floor. It was Daniel's slight voice that snapped her out of her rage.

"Kayla?" Daniel had said, then ran into her arms. She rubbed his back and assured him that the whole situation was over. When the cops stormed through the door, they saw Keisha balled up in the corner sobbing lightly, her arms secured around her chest, her wedding dress gathered about her. She babbled incoherently as she was handcuffed and then escorted to a waiting squad car.

Kayla closed her eyes, said a silent prayer of thanks, then smiled broadly when she, Daniel and Allen walked out of his house. The trio was immediately greeted by their family and friends.

Kayla had stayed with Allen and Daniel up to the day before their wedding. She had decided to rent out her condo and move in with them, but insisted on sleeping in Allen's home office. Together they continued to plan their wedding, with Jeanette coming by daily to assist. When the day of the wedding arrived, it was Jeanette who greeted Kayla when she awoke.

"My baby girl." She sat on the bed. "I was such a fool. I truly realized that when that deranged woman was holding you hostage. All I kept thinking of was that she was going to hurt my baby. That's when it hit me. I had missed so much. I should have fought harder. I shouldn't have left in the first place. Now, the only thing that could pull me away from you and Laura is the good Lord himself." Jeanette kissed her on her cheek.

"I forgive you mother, I really do," Kayla said as the two of them cried tears of joy. She could feel Jeanette's own tears — her body heaved as the two cried.

Joseph knocked on the door. "Hey, is there any room in here for the father of the bride?"

Kayla climbed out of bed and ran into her father's arms.

"Jeanette, let me talk to Kayla a minute."

Jeanette smiled and walked silently out of the room.

Kayla and her father sat on the bed. She watched slight tears form in the corners of his eyes as he told her about love lost and found, and admonished her never to give up on love. He ended by saying, "Love Allen as he does you." He kissed her on her forehead, then left.

Laura entered the room next. They hadn't spoken since the incident with Keisha.

"I'm only going to say this," Laura sighed. "I was wrong, so very wrong, Kayla. You are more than capable of handling your life." She took her sister's hand in hers, then pulled her into an embrace. "Hey, no tears. We've got a wedding to go to," Laura sniffed.

Kayla nodded, wiped the tears from her eyes and prepared for her wedding. As she stepped into her floor-length gown, she thought of Allen and Daniel. How close she came to losing them both.

When she stepped into the vestibule of the small church, her arm entwined with her father's, she looked at the small group gathered. Kayla looked up at her father. "I forgive you daddy." He kissed her on the cheek, then proceeded to escort her down the aisle.

Once at the altar, her eyes fell upon Tim first. He smiled at her — then glanced over at Amina standing a short dis-

tance to his right. Then she saw Allen. He was truly handsome as he stood, waiting for her, dressed in a simple black
tuxedo, its white shirt fastened at the neck with a black onyx
button cover. Next to him stood Daniel, in a matching tux;
his wide grin warmed her. Kayla thought of how much she
truly loved them both and would spend the rest of her life
making sure that they knew it.

INDIGO

Winter & Spring 2002

❦ March

No Apologies	Seressia Glass	$8.95
An Unfinished Love Affair	Barbara Keaton	$8.95

❦ April

Jolie's Surrender	Edwina Martin-Arnold	$8.95
Promises to Keep	Alicia Wiggins	$8.95

❦ May

Magnolia Sunset	Giselle Carmichael	$8.95
Once in a Blue Moon	Dorianne Cole	$9.95

❦ June

Still Waters Run Deep	Leslie Esdaile	$9.95
Everything but Love	Natalie Dunbar	$8.95

Indigo After Dark Vol. V		$14.95
Brown Sugar Diaries Part II	Dolores Bundy	

OTHER INDIGO TITLES

A Dangerous Deception	J.M. Jeffries	$8.95
A Dangerous Love	J.M. Jeffries	$8.95
After The Vows (Summer Anthology)	Leslie Esdaile	$10.95
	T.T. Henderson	
	Jacquelin Thomas	
Again My Love	Kayla Perrin	$10.95
A Lighter Shade of Brown	Vicki Andrews	$8.95
All I Ask	Barbara Keaton	$8.95
A Love to Cherish	Beverly Clark	$8.95
Ambrosia	T.T. Henderson	$8.95
And Then Came You	Dorothy Love	$8.95
Best of Friends	Natalie Dunbar	$8.95
Bound by Love	Beverly Clark	$8.95
Breeze	Robin Hampton	$10.95
Cajun Heat	Charlene Berry	$8.95
Careless Whispers	Rochelle Alers	$8.95
Caught in a Trap	Andree Michele	$8.95
Chances	Pamela Leigh Starr	$8.95
Dark Embrace	Crystal Wilson Harris	$8.95
Dark Storm Rising	Chinelu Moore	$10.95
Eve's Prescription	Edwinna Martin Arnold	$8.95
Everlastin' Love	Gay G. Gunn	$8.95
Gentle Yearning	Rochelle Alers	$10.95
Glory of Love	Sinclair LeBeau	$10.95
Illusions	Pamela Leigh Starr	$8.95
Indiscretions	Donna Hill	$8.95
Interlude	Donna Hill	$8.95
Intimate Intentions	Angie Daniels	$8.9

Kiss or Keep	Debra Phillips	$8.95
Love Always	Mildred E. Riley	$10.95
Love Unveiled	Gloria Green	$10.95
Love's Deception	Charlene Berry	$10.95
Mae's Promise	Melody Walcott	$8.95
Midnight Clear (Anthology)	Leslie Esdaile	$10.95
	Gwynne Forster	
	Carmen Green	
	Monica Jackson	
Midnight Magic	Gwynne Forster	$8.95
Midnight Peril	Vicki Andrews	$10.95
Naked Soul	Gwynne Forster	$8.95
No Regrets	Mildred E. Riley	$8.95
Nowhere to Run	Gay G. Gunn	$10.95
Passion	T.T. Henderson	$10.95
Past Promises	Jahmel West	$8.95
Path of Fire	T.T. Henderson	$8.95
Picture Perfect	Reon Carter	$8.95
Pride & Joi	Gay G. Gunn	$8.95
Quiet Storm	Donna Hill	$10.95
Reckless Surrender	Rochelle Alers	$8.95
Rendezvous with Fate	Jeanne Sumerix	$8.95
Rooms of the Heart	Donna Hill	$8.95
Shades of Desire	Monica White	$8.95
Sin	Crystal Rhodes	$8.95
So Amazing	Sinclair LeBeau	$8.95
Somebody's Someone	Sinclair LeBeau	$8.95
Soul to Soul	Donna Hill	$8.95
Subtle Secrets	Wanda Y. Thomas	$8.95
Sweet Tomorrows	Kimberley White	$8.95

The Price of Love	*Sinclair LeBeau*	*$8.95*
The Reluctant Captive	*Joyce Jackson*	*$8.95*
The Missing Link	*Charlyne Dickerson*	*$8.95*
Truly Inseparable	*Wanda Y. Thomas*	*$8.95*
Unconditional Love	*Alicia Wiggins*	*$8.95*
Whispers in the Night	*Dorothy Love*	*$8.95*
Whispers in the Sand	*LaFlorya Gauthier*	*$10.95*
Yesterday is Gone	*Beverly Clark*	*$8.95*
Yesterday's Dreams, Tomorrow's Promises	*Reon Laudat*	*$8.95*
Your Precious Love	*Sinclair LeBeau*	*$8.95*

You may order on-line at www.genesis-press.com, by phone at 1-888-463-4461, or mail the order-form in the back of this book.

Love Spectrum Romance

Romance across the culture lines

Forbidden Quest	Dar Tomlinson	$10.95
Designer Passion	Dar Tomlinson	$8.95
Fate	Pamela Leigh Starr	$8.95
Against the Wind	Gwynne Forster	$8.95
From The Ashes	Kathleen Suzanne Jeanne Summerix	$8.95
Heartbeat	Stephanie Bedwell-Grime	$8.95
My Buffalo Soldier	Barbara B. K. Reeves	$8.95
Meant to Be	Jeanne Sumerix	$8.95
A Risk of Rain	Dar Tomlinson	$8.95

Indigo After Dark

erotica beyond sensuous

Indigo After Dark Vol. I $10.95
     In Between the Night   Angelique
     Midnight Erotic Fantasies Nia Dixon

Indigo After Dark Vol. II $10.95
     The Forbidden Art of Desire Cole Riley
     Erotic Short Stories   Dolores Bundy

Indigo After Dark Vol. III $10.95
     Impulse   Montana Blue
     Pant   Boca Morena

ORDER FORM

Mail to: Genesis Press, Inc.
315 3rd Avenue North
Columbus, MS 39701

Name _____

Address _____

City/State _____ Zip _____

Telephone _____

Ship to (if different from above)

Name _____

Address _____

City/State _____ Zip _____

Telephone _____

Qty	Author	Title	Price	Total

Use this order form, or call
1-888-INDIGO-1

Total for books _____

Shipping and handling:
$3 first book, $1 each
additional book _____

Total S & H _____

Total amount enclosed _____

MS residents add 7% sales tax